**Gun**

"You tellin' me what

"I am," Clint said. ... give the man his
wallet and go back into your room."

Clint was in an even worse mood than he'd been in
when he'd left the comfort of his own bed. All he needed
now was to have to kill this jasper and then have to explain
it to the local law.

But the situation looked like it was beyond talking out.

"Put the wallet and the gun down," Clint said.

Dolan turned his head to look at Clint again. The tension in his shoulder gave away what his next move was going to be. He whirled on Clint, bringing the gun around . . .

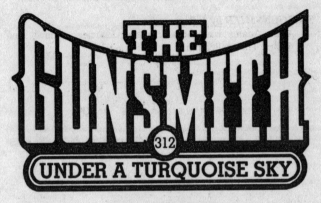

# THE GUNSMITH

## 312

## UNDER A TURQUOISE SKY

### J. R. ROBERTS

JOVE BOOKS, NEW YORK

**THE BERKLEY PUBLISHING GROUP**
**Published by the Penguin Group**
**Penguin Group (USA) Inc.**
**375 Hudson Street, New York, New York 10014, USA**
Penguin Group (Canada), 90 Eglinton Avenue East, Suite 700, Toronto, Ontario M4P 2Y3, Canada
(a division of Pearson Penguin Canada Inc.)
Penguin Books Ltd., 80 Strand, London WC2R 0RL, England
Penguin Group Ireland, 25 St. Stephen's Green, Dublin 2, Ireland (a division of Penguin Books Ltd.)
Penguin Group (Australia), 250 Camberwell Road, Camberwell, Victoria 3124, Australia
(a division of Pearson Australia Group Pty. Ltd.)
Penguin Books India Pvt. Ltd., 11 Community Centre, Panchsheel Park, New Delhi—110 017, India
Penguin Group (NZ), 67 Apollo Drive, Rosedale, North Shore 0632, New Zealand
(a division of Pearson New Zealand Ltd.)
Penguin Books (South Africa) (Pty.) Ltd., 24 Sturdee Avenue, Rosebank, Johannesburg 2196,
South Africa

Penguin Books Ltd., Registered Offices: 80 Strand, London WC2R 0RL, England

This is a work of fiction. Names, characters, places, and incidents either are the product of the author's imagination or are used fictitiously, and any resemblance to actual persons, living or dead, business establishments, events, or locales is entirely coincidental.

UNDER A TURQUOISE SKY

A Jove Book / published by arrangement with the author

PRINTING HISTORY
Jove edition / December 2007

ISBN: 978-0-515-14387-4

JOVE®
Jove Books are published by The Berkley Publishing Group,
a division of Penguin Group (USA) Inc.,
375 Hudson Street, New York, New York 10014.
JOVE is a registered trademark of Penguin Group (USA) Inc.
The "J" design is a trademark belonging to Penguin Group (USA) Inc.

PRINTED IN THE UNITED STATES OF AMERICA

10  9  8  7  6  5  4  3  2  1

# ONE

Kingman, Arizona, was a hub of the mining activity going on in the surrounding Cerbat Mountains. When General George Markstein alighted from the stagecoach in front of the Kingman Hotel, he had in his jacket pocket a large piece of rough turquoise, which had come out of those mountains. That piece of rock had brought him from New York all the way to Arizona, where he hoped to mine a fortune's worth of the beautiful blue stones, which he would then ship back East and sell.

"Help ya with yer bag, mister?" a drunken man offered.

Markstein looked the man over. Certainly inebriated and filthy, but somehow fit looking, he decided to cultivate the man immediately. He was, after all, an easterner, and he was going to need help integrating himself into the western lifestyle.

"Very well, my good man," he said, handing his suitcase over. "I'm going into this hotel."

"Best place in town to stay, mister," the man said. "Come on, I'll show ya the front desk."

"What's your name?" Markstein asked.

"Wooster," the drunk answered, "Charlie Wooster."

"Your name is Charles, then?" Markstein asked. "Very well, Charles, lead on."

"This way," Wooster said.

"That him?" Aaron Edwards asked as the man from the East followed the town drunk, Wooster, into the hotel.

"That's him," Carl Breckens said around a big plug of chewing tobacco. He spit and some of the juice dripped down his chin and onto his chest. He didn't notice.

"Well, when do we do it?" Edwards asked.

"When the time is right."

"And when will that be?" the other man asked. "I want the rest of my money."

"You ain't gonna get no more money if we don't get away with it," Breckens told him. "We got to be smart and wait."

"Why does bein' smart always seem to mean we gotta wait?" Edwards demanded.

"Because movin' too fast without thinkin' things through is dumb," Breckens said.

Edwards fumed inwardly. Breckens was always calling him stupid. Well, how smart was it to dribble tobacco juice down your chin? he wondered.

"I wired ahead for the best room in your hotel," Markstein said.

"Sir," the clerk said, "we're very full and I did save you a room."

"Is it the best room in the hotel?"

"Well, no . . ."

"I demand to see your manager."

"Sir, I am the manager," the man said. "Jackson Boggs, at your service." The man was small, about five-five, a faded looking fifty-year-old in a suit that had seen better days.

"Well, apparently not," Markstein said. He stared down

at the smaller man from his full six-foot-four, wearing his own three piece suit that had cost more than all of the furniture in the lobby combined. "Or I'd have the best room."

"Well, sir . . . we did have that room saved, but we had a surprise guest . . ."

"And he got my room?"

"Well, sir, he's—"

"Never mind," Markstein said, holding up his hand. "I don't care who he is. Just tell me what room he is in and I'll take care of the matter myself."

"But sir—"

"What room is he in?"

"Five."

"And what room are you putting me in?"

"Ten."

"Right down the hall?"

"Yes, sir."

"Good," Markstein said, "then he won't have far to go to switch rooms."

"Sir—"

"Once the switch has been made, I'll inform you and you can have your maid bring fresh sheets and towels."

"Maid?" the man asked.

"Charles," Markstein said, turning to the man who was still holding his suitcase, "take my suitcase to room ten."

"Yes, sir!" Charlie Wooster figured he was finally going to get paid.

"Towels?" Boggs said.

"And as soon as you fetch the remainder of my luggage from the stagecoach," Markstein said, "I will reward you."

"Th-the rest?" Wooster asked, as Markstein started up the steps.

"Fresh sheets?" Boggs repeated.

"Hop to, gentlemen," Markstein said. "We don't have all day. I have matters to attend to."

# TWO

As Wooster dragged the last piece of luggage—a large, heavy trunk—into room ten, Markstein stared out his window at the street below. It was midday and the street was busy with pedestrians, wagons and buckboards, all negotiating deep mudholes and ruts. Looking down at his own boots, he saw that they were already coated with mud.

"That's it, boss," Wooster said.

Markstein turned and looked at the sweating man—perspiring as much from the need for alcohol as from the effort of dragging the suitcases and trunk up the stairs.

"Excellent," Markstein said. He reached into his pocket, came out with a dollar, and then a second one as an afterthought. "Here you go, my good man."

Wooster put out his hand and Markstein placed the money in his grimy palm.

Thank you, boss," Wooster said. "Thank you kindly. You need any more ... help ... you just let ol' Charlie Wooster ... know." The drunkard was still panting, trying to catch his breath. Markstein hoped he wouldn't have a heart attack before he got to a saloon.

As Wooster started to leave, Markstein said, "Wait a moment."

"Boss?" Wooster said.

"What was that other room number the desk clerk mentioned?" Markstein asked.

"Room five, boss."

"Thank you."

"But I wouldn't go there if I were you," Wooster added.

"Oh? Why not?"

Wooster looked around, then stepped back into the room, closing the door behind him. Markstein suddenly became aware of the stench of the man's unwashed body.

"The man in that room won't take kindly to bein' asked ta move."

"Why not?" Markstein asked. "I'll make it worth his while."

A crafty look came into Wooster's eyes.

"You mean money?"

"Of course I mean money," Markstein said.

"Boss . . . are you a rich man?"

Markstein opened his mouth to answer, then thought better of it.

"Well, no, I am not a rich man," he said, carefully, "but I am willing to pay for what I want."

"And you want that room?"

"If it is the best room in the hotel," Markstein said, "I want it."

"Why don't you let me talk to him for ya?" Charlie Wooster asked. "Maybe I can—"

"Nonsense," Markstein said, cutting him off. "I do my own negotiating."

"Forgive me," Wooster said, "but negotiating in the East is real different from doin' it in the West. I think I'd have a better chance of convincing him to switch rooms with you."

"And you'd like to be paid for this?"

"Only if it's worth somethin' ta ya," Wooster said.

"Well," Markstein said, "my comfort is very important to me. If you can convince him, I would make it worth your while."

"That's great," Wooster said. "I'll go talk to him right now."

Markstein was impressed that, as much as the man obviously needed a drink, he was willing to do that first.

He looked around his small room with its thin mattress in distaste and said, "I'll wait right here."

The man in room five grabbed the woman by the ankles, spread her legs wide and brutally plunged his rigid penis into her. She gasped and grabbed a handful of sheets with each hand and grunted each time he drove into her. He had been brutal with her ever since she first entered the room, and she was going to have the bruises to prove it, but this was what she got paid for. Besides, she kind of liked it . . .

He also grunted as he fucked her, but he sounded more like a bull. Abruptly he released her ankles and withdrew, telling her, "Turn over," and then flipping her roughly.

"Lift your ass!" he commanded.

She did so and he slapped it hard, more than once. She was tall and thin, not much meat on her, but he got a satisfactory smacking sound as his hand reddened her ass cheeks. She yelped each time he hit her, then gasped again as he reached up between her legs and poked his fingers inside of her. His skin was hard and rough as he probed her, but even though it felt uncomfortable she wet his hand with her juices, which she couldn't control. The more it hurt, the wetter she got, which made her his kind of woman.

Once she was soaking wet, he removed his fingers, moved up close behind her, took hold of her hips and probed between her legs with his long dick. When he found her moist hole, he poked in again and then began to fuck her from behind that way. She found his rhythm and began

to rock back against him so that the room filled not only with
the squeaking sound of the bed, but also the sound of slapping flesh. In addition, the gun and holster hanging on the
bedpost began to rock, creating a clinking noise to go
along with the rest.

The man was gathering momentum, driving toward his
climax when the knock came at the door. He withdrew
from the woman in anger, grabbed the gun from the holster
and stormed to the door naked. There was no way he could
fuck while somebody was knocking at the door, and that
somebody was gonna pay for the interruption.

# THREE

When the door opened, the man stuck his gun in Charlie Wooster's face. That concerned Wooster more than the other part of the man's body that was sticking out. "This better be good." Then he recognized the drunk. "Wooster, what the hell—"

"Sorry, Mr.—"

"What do you want?" the man demanded. He was still angry, but removed the gun from the center of Wooster's face.

"Well, sir, there's this fella who just got in town? From back East? And he, uh, sorta wants this room."

"My room?"

"Yes, sir."

"What for?"

"Well, uh, seems this is the best room in the hotel."

The man frowned, then ducked his head into the room for a minute before ducking it out again.

"Looks just about like any other room," he said.

"It's, uh, bigger."

"That right?"

"I guess."

"Well, you tell this fella from back East he's outta luck." The man started to withdraw and close the door.

"He says he'll, uh, pay."

The door stopped, opened, and the man stuck his head out again.

"He'll pay?"

"Yes, sir."

"How much?"

"I dunno," Wooster said, "but he's got lots of money."

The man squinted at him.

"And you want a finder's fee, right?"

"Well . . ."

The man stuck his gun back in Wooster's face, causing Wooster to lose all the saliva in his mouth.

"You tell the man to come and talk to me himself," he said, "and to bring his wallet."

"But . . . I can make a good deal."

"Do what I say, Wooster."

The drunk became indignant.

"B-but . . . you're tryin' ta cut me out."

"You got that right, Charlie," the man said, "Now do what I tell ya."

"No!" Wooster said. "I got a right—"

"You got a right to this!" the man said. He reversed the gun and struck Wooster right on the bridge of the nose.

Markstein answered the knock on his door and found Wooster standing there, blood dripping down his face from his nose and dropping onto the floor. He leaped back.

"Jesus Christ, man!" he said. "What happened to you?"

"Uh, the man says you should ask him about the room yerself," Wooster said, "but I wouldn't, mister—"

"He did that to you?"

"Yeah, he hit me with his gun."

"This is preposterous," Markstein said. "This is no way to conduct business."

"Uh, he ain't a businessman, mister—"

"Excuse me," Markstein said, barging past Wooster.

"He's got a woman in there with him," Wooster warned. "He ain't gonna take kindly ta bein' interrupted."

"I'll reason with the man," Markstein said confidently.

He stopped in front of room five, heard some squeaking and grunting sounds from inside, but knocked on the door nevertheless.

The man and the woman had the bedpost banging on the wall pretty good when there was a knock at the door again.

"Forget it," she told the man, but he withdrew from her, grabbed his gun and stormed to the door.

"What?" he demanded, extending both the gun and his dick.

"Good God, man!" George Markstein exclaimed, jumping back. He hardly noticed the gun as the man's glistening, raging, blood-engorged dick alarmed him.

"Are you the dandy from the East who wants my room?" the man demanded.

Markstein, trying to avert his eyes from the male nudity, looked past him and saw the thin blonde on the bed with large, pear-shaped breasts, watching them impatiently. She seemed to have some welts and bruises on her body, as well.

"My God, is that . . . is that a prostitute?" he asked.

"That's a whore," the man answered. "Don't they have whores back East where you come from?"

"I suppose—"

"Look, I'm busy." He waved his gun in the man's face to get his attention away from the whore. "You got an offer to make me, make it and be done with it."

"An offer—"

"You want my room, right?"

"Oh, yes, of course," Markstein said. "There really was no need for violence. Poor Mr. Wooster's nose—"

"Violence is the only way to get things done, friend," the man said. "And if you don't start sayin' somethin' I wanna hear, you're gonna find out the hard way."

He extended his gun again, and cocked the hammer back. It got very quiet in the hall.

# FOUR

All Clint Adams wanted when he rode into Kingman was about ten or twelve or fourteen hours of sleep. He'd arrived after dark and hadn't bothered with a drink, a meal or a bath. He'd just flopped onto the bed and fallen asleep. He hoped to wake up sometime during the afternoon, but of his own accord, not to a racket out in the hallway.

When the shouting and slamming against walls got to be too much to bear, he practically leaped from the bed and rushed to the door.

"A thousand dollars," Mike Dolan said to George Markstein.

"That's ridiculous!"

"You want the room, don't you?" Dolan demanded. "That's the price. Take it or leave it."

"I will give you a hundred dollars and no more, sir!" Markstein said. "You will find that a fair price."

"Mike!" the whore, Loretta, called from inside the room. "We ain't done, are we?"

"No, we ain't done," Dolan shouted. "Just hold on. Me and this dandy are doin' business." He turned his attention back to Markstein.

Wooster watched the action from down the hall, standing inside Markstein's room, sticking his head out. He hoped the dandy wouldn't get killed, because he figured the man was good for some more drinking money.

"You can take your hundred dollars and shove it up your ass," Dolan said. "A thousand is the price."

"You are being unreasonable, sir."

Dolan put his hand against Markstein's chest and pushed. The man bounced off the wall on the other side of the hall. Dolan followed him out, and put his forearm beneath the man's chin and his gun beneath the man's jaw.

"A thousand," he said, "or I'll blow your head off right now."

"Th-this is robbery!" Markstein said,

"You interrupted me, friend," Dolan said. "That's worth a thousand right there."

"B-but—"

"Come on, come on," Dolan said, "I got me an impatient whore waitin' on me."

"I—I don't carry that much money on me."

"You don't, huh?" Dolan took his forearm away, began patting the Easterner down for his wallet. "Come on, where's your wallet?"

"Here now!" Markstein said. "I'll put up with no more of this."

As Mike Dolan pulled Markstein's wallet from his jacket pocket, the man made a grab for it. Dolan slammed his gun down on Markstein's head, driving the man to the floor. He was bloodied but not unconscious.

The door to room seven opened and Clint Adams stepped out. He was still wearing his gun because he'd been too tired to remove it and had fallen asleep with it on.

"What the hell is going on out here!"

Mike Dolan turned toward Clint's voice, tearing his

eyes from the many bills he'd seen in George Markstein's wallet.

"Go back into your room, friend," he shouted. "This ain't none of your affair."

"You woke me up," Clint said. "That makes it my affair."

"He's robbing me!" the bloodied man on the floor said.

"No robbery goin' on here," Dolan said. "Me and this feller are just doin' some business."

"What kind of business?"

"He's payin' me a thousand dollars to switch rooms with him."

"That's not true!" Markstein cried. "I offered him a hundred—"

Dolan kicked Markstein in the chest absently, just hard enough to shut the man up.

"Like I told ya, mister," he said, still delving into Markstein's wallet. "Not your business."

"If you'd kept it down, I'd agree with you," Clint said, "but your noise brought me out here, so now I'd suggest you give the man his wallet and go back into your room."

"What?" Dolan froze, wallet in one hand, gun in the other.

"Don't even think about turning to face me with that gun in your hand, mister," Clint said. "I'm not in a good mood when somebody wakes me up from a deep sleep."

"Friend," Dolan said, "if I turn toward you with my gun, you're gonna end up in an even deeper sleep."

"Don't try it," Clint said. "I just got to town last night and I haven't had anything to eat yet."

"That a fact?"

"It is," Clint said, "and I'm not killing on an empty stomach."

"Yer a funny guy."

"I told you," Clint said. "Not so funny when somebody

wakes me up. So why don't we all go back to our own rooms?"

"You tellin' me what to do?"

"I am," Clint said. "I'm telling you to give the man his wallet and go back into your room."

"Mike!" Loretta wailed from inside the room. "Come on, do like he says. I ain't done yet."

"Shut up, Loretta!" Dolan shouted. "Mister, take yer own advice and go into your room before you get hurt, you hear?"

Wooster, watching from down the hall, didn't know who the man from room seven was, but he sure hoped he could draw against an already palmed gun, or Mike Dolan would kill him for sure. Still, as long as the Easterner on the floor didn't catch a stray bullet, he'd be happy.

God, he was thirsty. He never should've gotten involved in the room switch. Should have just gone and had that drink.

From the floor, with blood in his eyes, George Markstein couldn't be sure what was happening. He was also holding his chest where Mike Dolan had kicked him. He didn't know who the man from room seven was, but he seemed to be the Easterner's only chance of coming out of this alive.

Damned hotel! They should have held that room for him like they were supposed to.

Loretta had other business to do that day. She needed Mike Dolan to finish fucking her and beating on her so she could get paid and go back to the whorehouse. One of her best customers was coming in this evening, and she wanted to have a bath first.

She didn't know who the other man in the hall was, but

she hoped he wouldn't kill Mike Dolan before she could get paid.

Clint was in an even worse mood than he'd been when he'd left the comfort of the hotel bed. All he needed now was to have to kill this jasper and then have to explain it to the local law.

But the situation looked like it was beyond talking it out.

"Put the wallet and the gun down," Clint said.

Dolan turned his head to look at Clint again. The tension in his shoulder gave away what his next move was going to be. He whirled on Clint, bringing the gun around. Clint's hand moved like a blur. He drew his gun and blew a hole in Mike Dolan's chest.

Dolan flew backward, his gun and the wallet flying from his hands. As he landed on his back, his gun hit the floor but the wallet landed on top of its owner, Markstein, who grabbed it and then covered his head with both hands.

Wooster couldn't believe what he'd seen from down the hall. He'd never seen a man draw his gun that fast.

The whore, Loretta, came to the doorway, one hand scratching her crotch and the other cupping one of her big breasts. She looked down at Dolan, knew he was dead, and then looked at Clint.

"Guess I ain't gettin' paid today," she said, then added, "unless—"

"Try him," Clint said, pointing at the man on the floor. "He looks like he needs some tender loving."

He backed into his room and closed the door. Let somebody else clean up the mess.

# FIVE

When the knock came at his door, it was no surprise, but at least now he had splashed some water on his face and was awake. He opened the door and found himself facing a man wearing a sheriff's badge.

"Sheriff."

"Your name Clint Adams?" the man asked.

"That's me."

The sheriff had a craggy face behind a bushy mustache, and looked like a man who had been wearing tin for about twenty years. Clint had no desire to give him a hard time.

"The Gunsmith, right? No joke?" the lawman asked.

"No joke."

"Well, based on what the witnesses said, I'm inclined to believe you," the sheriff said. "Of course, two of the witnesses are a drunk and a whore."

"And the man with the wallet?"

"He's in room ten," the sheriff said. "Says you saved him from bein' robbed, and probably saved his life."

"I don't know, you tell me," Clint said. "Were you acquainted with the dead man?"

"Mike Dolan? Everybody around here was acquainted

with Mike Dolan. He needed killin'. Yeah, you probably saved the fella's life."

Clint looked out into the hall where a couple of men were removing the body.

"My name's Cafferty," the lawman said. He put his hand out for Clint to shake.

"Sheriff Cafferty." Clint shook the man's hand.

"Fella down the hall whose life you saved wants to thank you," the sheriff said.

"That's it?" Clint asked. "You're not going to ask for my gun? Tell me to leave town? Ask me when I got here, what I want here?"

"Desk clerk says you got here last night, all you wanted to do was sleep," Cafferty said. "Seems to me the commotion in the hall woke you up and you came out just at the right time."

"Or wrong time."

Cafferty shrugged.

"That depends on how you look at it, I guess," he said. "Wrong for you, right for the dude from the East. He's in room ten, by the way. Wants you to stop in."

"How is he?"

"Battered, bruised," Cafferty said. "The doc's in with him now, patchin' him up."

"I'll stop in."

"By the way," the lawman asked. "What are you doin' in town?"

"Just passing through, Sheriff," Clint said. "Just passing through."

After the lawman left, Clint closed his door, locked it, and walked to room ten. He knocked on the door and heard someone shout "Come!"

As he entered, the man on the bed pushed the doctor away and said, "That's the man who saved my life! Come in, come in, my friend."

Clint looked at the sawbones, who had an exasperated look on his heavily lined face. He got the same feeling from the doctor that he got from the sheriff: that they'd been here awhile and seen a lot.

"How's he doing?" Clint asked.

"He's got a bump on his head," the doctor said, "and he's ornery. I'm Doc Miller."

"Clint Adams."

"Mr. Adams," the man on the bed said, "my name is George Markstein and I owe you my life."

"Mr. Markstein," Clint said, "you really don't owe anything, not for killing a man—"

"That man needed killing," Markstein said. "He was . . . brutal. Did you see the marks on the woman?"

"On the whore?" Clint asked.

"Whore or not, he needn't have marked her that way," Markstein said. "Any man who would treat a woman that way deserves to be shot."

"Well, I just wish I hadn't had to do it," Clint said. "I only came out of my room because the noise woke me up."

"And lucky for me that you did," Markstein said. He had a bandage on his head, and there was a little blood seeping through. "I hope you'll let me repay you in some way."

"I think you'd better just concentrate on healing up, sir," Clint said. "I just dropped by to see how you were doing."

"I'm doing quite well, thanks to you."

"And the doctor."

"Yes, of course," Markstein said. "Will you dine with me, sir? Perhaps tomorrow evening? My treat, of course."

"You don't have to—"

"I'd like to talk with you about a business proposition."

"Business? What business are you in, Mr. Markstein?"

"Stone," the man said, "precious stones."

The doctor was closing his bag and said, "You must be here about the mines, then."

"Doctor, how much do I owe you?" Markstein asked.

"You two settle up," Clint said. "I just got to town last night and I haven't eaten a thing yet. I'm going to go out and find a restaurant."

"Find a good one and we can go there tomorrow," Markstein said. "I believe I can make it worth your while."

"Sure," Clint said, "why not? I'll see you tomorrow evening, Mr. Markstein."

"Now, Doctor," the man was saying as Clint left, "about your fee . . ."

# SIX

Clint found a place for a decent steak and a good cup of coffee, then found a saloon with cold beer and poker. He was definitely unhappy about having had to kill Mike Dolan, but everywhere he went he heard people talking about it, saying that "finally" somebody had killed Dolan, who "needed" it.

The saloon he settled in was called the Nighthawk Saloon. Kingman, which just several years earlier had been a one-tent, one-saloon, one-horse town, was growing, but the Nighthawk had been one of the first saloons and was not only still around, but was prospering.

He could still smell the new wood scent as he entered. While the long bar was scarred in places, they obviously were not years worth of scars. With a cold beer in hand he turned to examine the room. It had everything it was supposed to have—games, girls, music. And in one corner, eyeing Clint Adams, it had Carl Breckens and Aaron Edwards . . .

"It's a damn good thing we didn't go into that hotel today," Edwards said. "Who knew the goddamned Gunsmith would be in there. We'd both be dead by now."

"And why didn't we go in?" Breckens asked.

"I know, I know," Edwards said, "it was because you wouldn't let us. You was right, we got to go slow and think first."

"You can go slow," Breckens said, "but the thinking is gonna be up to me. Right?"

"Yeah, right."

"So why don't you go slowly up to the bar and get us two more beers," Breckens said. "And try not to get killed while you're doin' it."

At the far end of the bar to his left Clint saw somebody he recognized, but he couldn't quite place him. It took him a few moments, but then he realized he'd seen the man in the hallway near his room in the hotel during all the ruckus.

He called the bartender over and asked, "Who's that fella down there? At the end of the bar, by the window?"

"Him?" the bartender said. "That's Wooster, Charlie Wooster. He's the town drunk."

"Town drunk?"

"Well, as much of one as we got," the man added. "He ain't fallin' down drunk all the time, but he does odd jobs for whiskey money."

Clint wondered what odd job Wooster had been doing in the hotel. Was he the go-between for the room switch that was supposed to take place? Did he get the amount of money wrong? At the moment the man was staring morosely into a glass of whiskey. Clint decided to leave him alone. He'd probably be able to get the whole story from Markstein at supper the next night, anyway.

"That an open game?" he asked the bartender, indicating a four-handed poker game that was taking place across the room.

"Yep. Anybody can play. Just walk over, sit down and put your money on the table."

Clint finished his beer first, because he didn't like to drink at the poker table. The he walked over and did like the bartender said, he just sat down and put his money on the table. They dealt him in the next hand.

"So what are we gonna do about him?" Edwards asked, indicating the poker-playing Gunsmith.

"Right now there's no reason to think he'll get in our way," Breckens said. "He just happened to be staying in a room down the hall from the commotion. But he did us a big favor."

"How do you figure that?"

"If he hadn't killed Dolan, then Dolan woulda killed our meal ticket," Breckens said. "That fella from the East would be dead right now."

"Jesus, you're right." He stared down into his fresh beer. "Maybe we need help with this?"

"You wanna split your end of the money?"

"Well, no, I just thought—"

"And I thought we said I was gonna do all the thinkin'," Breckens said.

"Yeah, well—"

"Yeah, well nothin', Aaron," Breckens said. "Just drink yer beer and shut up. I'll decide what we're gonna do and when we're gonna do it."

Breckens turned his attention away from his partner and back to Clint Adams, who seemed to have already accumulated some money in front of him.

Clint started doing well immediately because the other players at the table were so bad. Two of them were town merchants who played in the saloon regularly; the other two were like Clint, strangers passing through who were looking for a way to pass the time. They didn't seem to know each other, but Clint didn't like the coincidence of so many strangers at the same table, so he kept his eye on them.

As it turned out, that was a good idea.

Abruptly, the tide began to change in favor of the other two strangers. They weren't taking Clint's money, but they were doing a good job of taking money from the two merchants. It was a small-stakes game, but they were doing all right for themselves.

It soon became apparent to Clint that the two men were cheating. Obviously they knew each other, but each had come to the game separately. They probably traveled from town to town doing this.

Whenever one of them had a big hand, the other one began to build a pot by betting or raising with nothing, then getting out of the pot to leave it for his partner. They weren't so much cheating—nobody was bottom dealing or anything—but they were working in tandem, which was almost the same thing. Poker was a solitary game, not a team game. Playing it that way was frowned upon.

Clint was seated so he could see most of the room—he would not have joined the game otherwise—so he was immediately aware when the sheriff entered the saloon.

"Deal me out a couple of hands," he said, and stood up to go to the bar. That would make the two cheaters happy, because any time one of them had a hand, Clint would fold.

He went to the bar, where the sheriff had gotten himself a beer.

"Adams," Sheriff Cafferty said. "Found yourself a friendly game, I see."

"Maybe not so friendly," Clint said. He signaled the bartender for a beer.

"Whataya mean?"

"You know any of those players?"

"Two of 'em," Cafferty said. "Herb Olands owns the mercantile, and Jerry Hill runs the livery."

"I thought I recognized him," Clint said. His memory of arriving in town and putting Eclipse up at the livery was hazy. "You don't know the other two?"

"No better than I know you," the man said. "One rode into town early yesterday, the other the day before."

"The one who arrived first, he play any poker that you know of before the other one got here?" He asked the question knowing that a good lawman would be keeping an eye on strangers.

"Now that you mention it, no." Cafferty put his mug down on the bar. "Why? Are they cheatin'?"

"Depends on what you call cheating," Clint said. "They're playing together."

"I call that cheatin'. Can you prove it?"

"Watch the game when I go back," Clint said, and explained the scam to the lawman so he'd know what to look for.

Clint drank about half his beer and then returned to the game.

For the next hour or so the sheriff watched and saw what Clint Adams was talking about. The two merchants were being scammed, all right. Whenever the two strangers launched one of their bids, Clint would fold, sit back and wait. Finally, the sheriff had seen enough.

He walked over to the table and stood next to one of the strangers. After a moment, the man looked up at him.

"Looks like you're doin' pretty well for yourself," Cafferty said to the man.

"Uh, I'm doin' okay."

This was a man named Tim Bailey. He was in his late twenties. The other man was called Frank Anderson, in his forties and probably the mentor of the first man. He was obviously the more experienced of the two.

"Yeah, I'm doin' okay," Anderson said to the sheriff. "What about it, Sheriff?"

"I think you boys better come with me."

"What for?" Anderson asked.

"We're gonna have a little talk outside."

Bailey looked over at Anderson, who gave him an almost imperceptible nod.

"Okay," Anderson said. He looked at Bailey. "You see anythin' wrong with havin' a little talk, mister?"

"I guess not."

"I'll just gather up my money—" Anderson said, but the sheriff cut him off.

"That's okay," he said. "Just leave it on the table."

"What?"

"You won't need it."

"Whataya talkin' about?" Anderson demanded. "It's my money."

"Not anymore."

As if he thought nobody could see him, Bailey started picking up his money from the table. Cafferty dropped a hand on his shoulder.

"That's okay, friend," he said. "Just leave it."

Bailey tensed, looked across the table and made a big mistake. "Frank?" he said.

"Shut up!"

"Let's go, boys," the sheriff said. "We don't take kindly to poker cheats in this town. I think we'll just walk over to the livery, saddle your horses and you can be on your way."

"I'm not leavin' without my money," Anderson announced.

"It's not your money," Cafferty said, "it's theirs." He put his hand on his gun. "Now put your guns on the table and stand up."

Anderson dropped his right hand below the table, made like he was going to stand and then went for his gun.

# SEVEN

Clint drew his gun and pressed it to the side of the man's neck.

"I wouldn't." He lifted the man's gun from his holster. "Now do like the sheriff said and stand up. You, too," he said to the other man.

Bailey didn't try anything. He placed his gun on the table gently and stood up. The two merchants at the table just sat back and watched the proceedings, wide-eyed.

"I'll come back for the guns," Cafferty told the table.

"Want me to walk out with you?" Clint asked.

"No, thanks, Adams," Cafferty said. "You did enough spotting these two, and then saving my bacon when that one tried to go for his gun. I got it now."

"You?" Anderson said, "No wonder you kept sitting out."

"Let's go," Cafferty said.

The two men stood up and marched out of the saloon in front of Cafferty's gun.

"You knew they was cheatin'?" Jerry Hill asked.

"I caught on a little while into the game."

"And you told the sheriff?" Herb Olands said.

"That's right."

"Well," Hill said, "we're much obliged, mister."

"Don't mention it."

"But . . . what do we do with their money?" Hill asked.

"You fellas split it between you," Clint said, gathering up his own winnings. "After all, they took it from you."

He stood up, put his money in his pockets and said, "Good night to you."

As he left, the two men were divvying up the cash. Since it included the money from the two cheaters, it was probably one of the only times they had both come out ahead after a game.

Clint went to the bar and the bartender had a cold beer waiting for him.

"On the house," he said.

"Thanks."

"That was slick the way you spotted those two," someone came up alongside him and said.

"They weren't being very subtle about it," Clint replied. He picked up his beer and turned to face the owner of the voice. Earlier he'd noticed three girls working the floor—a blonde, a brunette and a redhead. The saloon seemed to like catering to all tastes. This was the redhead, the taller of the three, and the more bosomy. Much of her bosom was overflowing from the top of her green gown and he could see a sprinkling of freckles on the pale slopes.

"Also slick the way you drew your gun and saved the sheriff," she said.

"Probably saved him from having to kill that fella," he said. "I think the sheriff can handle himself."

"Oh, he sure can," she said. "He's been doin' it for as long as I been livin' here."

"And how long has that been?" Clint asked.

"A few months," she said. "Came in on a stage that left without me."

"And why was that?"

"I didn't have enough money to keep travelin'." She put her hand out. "My name's Shannon."

"Sure it is."

"No, really," she said.

He took her hand and said, "It's nice to meet you, Shannon . . ."

"O'Doyle," she said. "And that's real, too."

"Pleased to meet you," he said, releasing the long, graceful fingers of her hand. "My name is Clint Adams."

"I heard the sheriff say Adams," she said, "but . . . Clint?"

"That's right," he said. "Is that a problem?"

"Not for me," she said. "But I imagine it can be a problem for you, sometimes."

"It can be."

"Would you like to sit awhile and get acquainted?" she asked, touching his hand.

"Would you like a drink?"

"Just a whiskey," she said. She looked at the bartender and added, "And don't water it. I want to enjoy myself with Mr. Adams."

"Clint," he said. "My name is Clint."

She accepted her whiskey from the bartender, slipped her arm through Clint's and said, "I have a special table in the back."

As he walked across the saloon floor with Shannon on his arm, it was clear to him that she was the more popular of the three girls. Most of the men watched their progress, and the other two women frowned after them.

"It seems as if the other two girls don't like you," Clint said as they sat down, he with his back to the wall.

"They had the place all to themselves before I got here," she said. "Also, they're a little older and more experienced than I am."

"And that makes them less desirable, or more?" he asked.

"I guess that depends on who you ask," she said. "Some of the old-timers here have favorites. On the other hand, when the miners come to town they really don't care who they poke it in as long as they get to poke it."

"Seems to me you'd be a little more choosy, though."

"Oh, I am," she said. "That's why I'm sitting here with you. And that's also why I've decided that, when we finish our drinks, we should go back to your room and get acquainted there."

"Well," he said, "I really don't see why we even have to wait until we finish our drinks."

# EIGHT

Clint and Shannon were walking through the lobby on the way to the stairs when George Markstein came walking down.

"Mr. Adams," he said. "What a coincidence running into you. Young lady." He bowed slightly, and wasn't wearing a hat because of the bandage on his head.

"Mr. Markstein—"

"George, please," Markstein said.

"Hi, George," the redhead said. "I'm Shannon."

"I'm pleased to meet you, Shannon."

"Shouldn't you be in bed, George?" Clint asked.

"That's what the doctor said," Markstein replied, "but I feel like a walk."

"You're not going to find anyplace to eat this late, if that's what you're looking for."

"Not at all," Markstein said. "The doctor was kind enough to arrange to have some food brought in for me."

"I see. Then why would you be going out this late?" Clint asked the man curiously.

"I'm feeling cooped up in my room," Markstein said, "even though the hotel was kind enough to move me to room five."

"The bigger room? The one you got hurt over?"

"That's the one. Look, I'm just going out for some air," Markstein said. "Don't forget we have an appointment for supper tomorrow night."

"I haven't forgotten," Clint said, "but I don't think it's wise for you to go out on the street at this hour."

"Nonsense," Markstein said. "What could befall me just going out for a walk?"

"Honey," Shannon said, "you ever been in a mining town before?"

"No, I have not."

"That's obvious," she said, "or you wouldn't ask such a question. There's people on these streets who would kill you for your shoes."

"That's ridiculous—"

"You almost got killed over a room this afternoon," Clint reminded him.

Markstein looked frustrated.

"I just want to get some air, and perhaps smoke a cigar. Couldn't I just go out front safely?"

Clint looked at Shannon, who smiled.

"Go ahead," she said. "Give me your key and I'll wait in your room for you."

Clint handed his key over.

"You enjoy your cigar, George," she said to Markstein, touching his arm before she went up the stairs.

"What a delightful young woman," the easterner said. "Does this mean you'll be coming outside with me?"

"Just out front," Clint said. "A deep breath, a cigar, and then back to your room."

"Excellent!"

The two men walked outside and stopped on the boardwalk just in front of the hotel. Clint looked left and right, and found two wooden chairs they could use.

As they sat, Markstein pulled out a cigar.

"Would you like one?" he asked Clint.

"Not tonight, thanks." Clint could see that the cigars were expensive, and he didn't want the man to waste one on him.

Markstein lit his cigar with a wooden match, puffed at it until he had it going to his satisfaction, then shook the match out and tossed it into the street.

"Ah," he said, sitting back. "There's nothing like a good cigar."

"A good horse," Clint said, "a cold drink, a good woman . . . ah, a really good poker hand."

"I don't ride, or gamble," Markstein replied readily. "My days with women are over, and I prefer my liquor at room temperature. Therefore for me, it's the good cigar."

Clint couldn't argue with the man when he put it that way. He did wonder, though, if Markstein was done with women willingly or unwillingly. He didn't appear to be sixty yet—and Clint knew quite a few sixty-year-old men who still enjoyed women.

"Shall we discuss my business proposition tonight?" Markstein asked, then.

"No," Clint said. "I have other things on my mind. Besides, I have a place picked out for us tomorrow that has decent steaks and good coffee."

"Very well," Markstein said, "we'll wait. May I ask what your business is, Clint?"

Clint looked at the man, who was staring at the tip of his cigar as he waited for his answer. It seemed as if the man truly had no idea who Clint was. He found that refreshing.

"I'm a gunsmith," Clint said. "My business is guns."

"Ah, you work with your hands, then."

"Yes."

"And, I assume from what happened this evening, that you are fairly proficient with the tools of your trade?"

"Fairly," Clint said.

"Good, good."

Markstein continued to enjoy his cigar until it was about half gone. The street was dark and quiet except for the music coming from a couple of saloons down the street. Clint found his mind wandering to Shannon, who was waiting upstairs in his room.

Finally, Markstein said, "Well, I suppose it's time to turn in." He tossed half of his expensive cigar into the street, where Clint was sure someone like Charlie Wooster would find it and claim it as a prize.

"Thank you for the company, Clint," Markstein said, rising unsteadily. Clint grabbed his arm. "I seem to be a little dizzy."

"Come on," Clint said, "I'll get you back to your room."

"I seem to be relying on you quite a bit today," Markstein said. "I would say you are my first true friend in the West, Clint."

At that moment Clint didn't know if that was a good thing or a bad thing.

# NINE

When Clint entered his room, Shannon was on the bed, reading a book she had found in his saddlebags. It was *Treasure Island*, by Robert Louis Stevenson.

"This is very good."

She was still wearing her dress, but had discarded the shawl she'd thrown over it for the walk to the hotel.

"Yes, it is."

"Did you take care of your friend?" she asked. "Make sure he got to bed all right?"

"I got him to his room," he said. "He'll have to get himself into bed. We're not that good friends yet."

"When did you meet?"

"Only today."

"Oh," she said, setting the book aside, "then we're just as good friends as you and him?"

"Maybe," he said, removing his gun belt, "but we're about to get a lot more friendly."

In his room George Markstein removed his trousers, then reached into the pocket and took out the stone. It was rough, with brown veins. To the naked eye it might not have seemed like much, but Markstein came from a family of people who knew stones when they saw them. When this one was cleaned up, it would be breathtaking, and he knew where to get a lot more like it.

He set it on the table next to the bed. As he slid between the sheets, he thought that he had made some mistakes on his first day in Kingman—some mistakes since arriving in the West. He'd almost gotten killed today, but thanks to Clint Adams, he was alive to enjoy tomorrow.

He had decided that afternoon that if he was to see any more tomorrows, he was going to have to make sure Clint Adams was around him for a long time. And he didn't care how much it would cost him.

Across from the hotel both Breckens and Edwards stood in a store doorway, hidden by the shadows.

"We ain't goin' in tonight, are we?" Edwards asked.

"Not on your life," Breckens said. "Not while Clint Adams is inside."

"Then what are we doin' here?"

"Watchin'," Breckens said, "and thinkin'. But you know what? I don't need you for either one."

"So . . ."

"Go on back to the hotel and get some sleep," Breckens told him. "I won't be here much longer. I just got to figure some things out, and I can't do it with you breathin' down my neck."

"I can go to sleep?"

"That's what I said."

He didn't have to tell Edwards twice. The man quit the doorway and said he'd see Breckens in the morning.

Breckens waited until Edwards was out of sight, then left the doorway himself and went the other way, to the opposite end of town. He had a meeting and he was late.

• • •

"What took you?" the man demanded.

"I had to get rid of Edwards." Breckens sat down at the table across from his employer. They were in the tiny Saloon No. 1, the first saloon to have opened in Kingman. Very few people ever patronized it now, and the owner didn't much mind: He had other investments in town to be able to afford this conceit.

"So did he get to town?" the man asked.

"Got off the stage this afternoon."

"And is he dead?"

"Not yet."

The man sat back in his chair.

"I paid you to kill him."

"I know."

"And he's not dead."

"He will be."

"When?"

"Soon."

The man sat forward.

"I want it done tomorrow."

"That may not be possible."

"Why not? What's the holdup?"

"There's another player takin' a hand in the game."

The man raised his hand and said, "Save me your poker metaphors, Breckens."

"What?"

The man sighed.

"Go ahead—and stop chewing that damn tobacco while you're talking to me!"

Breckens stopped chewing, then spit the wad into his left hand. He looked around for someplace to put it, then simply dropped his hand down below table level. The thing sat in his hand like a hot turd. He'd pop it back into his mouth when he was done here. No use wasting good chaw.

"Now tell me," his employer said. "who is this new man you're talking about?"

# TEN

Clint peeled the dress from Shannon's body, doing it slowly and enjoying every inch of flesh that came into view. At the same time she removed his shirt and ran her hands over his chest.

When he had her naked on the bed, she suddenly seemed to get shy. It was probably because he wasn't paying. If she was with a man who was paying, speed would be the operative word, and she wouldn't have worried about how she looked—especially, as she'd explained to Clint earlier—if she was with a miner.

"What's wrong?" he asked, kissing her shoulder and fondling one of her full, round breasts.

"I have all these . . . ugly freckles," she said.

"Believe me," he said, licking the freckles that dappled the slopes of her breasts, "they're not ugly."

He thumbed her pale pink nipples. Actually, the nipple itself was a darker pink than the areola surrounding it. He ducked his head and concentrated on sucking them both until they were as hard as pebbles. She moaned and held the back of his head gently.

He stood up then to remove his pants, and she helped him, tugging them down so that his erection sprang free.

He kicked away the pants and underwear and moved closer to the bed. She rolled onto her stomach, reached beneath his penis to hold his testicles in one hand, and took him into her mouth. She sucked him wetly, moaning as he seemed to swell even larger in her mouth. She released him, used her tongue to just lick the tip, then that sensitive spot right underneath the tip, then slid the length of him back into her hot mouth. He moved his hips in unison with her sucking, then she abruptly released him, took hold of his cock and tugged him onto the bed with her . . .

"The Gunsmith," Carl Breckens's employer said. "You're sure?"

"Positive," Breckens said. "I heard the sheriff talkin' to him, callin' him by name."

The other man sat back and rubbed the side of his head, as if he had a pain there.

"What is he doing in town?" he asked aloud.

"Says he's passin' through."

"Could he be here working for Markstein?"

"The way it looked," Breckens said, "it don't seem like they knew each other before."

"That's good, that's good," the other man said. "Now it remains to be seen if they'll forge a relationship."

"Why would they?" Breckens asked. "What's the Gunsmith got in common with some dandy from back East?"

"That dandy just might decide to hire himself a gun, Breckens," the man said. "If he hires Adams, can you handle him?"

Breckens had already anticipated this question, and knew what his answer was going to be.

"For the right amount of money," he said, "I could handle the ghost of Wild Bill Hickok."

"Well," his employer said, "I'm going to take you at your

word, Breckens. No matter what happens, or who he hires, I want George Markstein dead."

Clint spread Shannon's pale thighs, pressed his face to her rust-colored pubic bush and proceeded to feast on her. She sighed and moaned as he used his tongue and lips to give her more pleasure than she'd felt in a long time. When she had sex, her own pleasure was the furthest thing from the mind of either participant. The man only wanted what he wanted, and she wanted to get it over with as soon as possible.

With Clint Adams she felt as if she were floating, and she wanted the feeling to go on forever. He seemed to care more for her pleasure than his own, which amazed her.

He slid his hands beneath her to cup her buttocks and lift her to his face so he could press his tongue deeper into her. As he licked and sucked her he moaned, and it was the sexiest sound she'd ever heard from a man. Just the sound of it made her even wetter.

"Don't stop," she implored him, reaching down to cup his head, "don't ever stop . . ."

Carl Breckens left Saloon No. 1 with some more of his employer's money in his pocket.

"If you need to hire somebody else to help you, then do it," the man had told him, pressing the money into his hands. "I need that man to be dead as soon as possible."

"I'm on it," Breckens promised him.

Now, as he left the saloon, he wondered what he should do about Clint Adams. He sure as hell would never face the man head-on. If—as his employer predicted—Markstein hired Adams, then the Gunsmith was going to face the same kind of death Wild Bill Hickok did years ago: a bullet in the back of the head.

All Carl Breckens had to decide was who was going to actually pull the trigger.

# ELEVEN

Clint had Shannon on all fours, and was enjoying the line of her back and the curve of her buttocks. He laid his rigid penis along the crack between her butt cheeks, then slid it down and around until he was nestled between her thighs. He poked further, found the moistness of her vagina and poked in. She gasped as he entered her slowly and then she began to move back and forth, taking him in and letting him out.

He took hold of her hips and worked her that way for while, then reached out one hand and took hold of her hair. She arched her back, her breath coming roughly as he increased the tempo. He reached around to touch her, run his hand over her, and she growled with the pleasure of it.

He was getting some pleasure himself, though. As he slid in and out of her, she'd tighten her thighs so that he was also getting some friction from there as well.

"Ooh, God," she said, "I've never been treated like this by a man in my life before."

He ran one hand along her back, then slapped one of her ass cheeks and said, "You've been with the wrong men, then."

"Mmm, you can say that again."

He continued to fuck her from behind, long, slow strokes, making her catch her breath each time he drove himself home. Eventually she went from being on her knees to having her face buried in a pillow, her ass lifted up high, her cries muffled, and when her orgasm came her entire body shook and vibrated and then she went completely slack beneath him.

"Jesus," she said, turning her head to the side so she wouldn't suffocate, "I really have been with the wrong men."

Later, after they had dozed for a while, Clint woke to the wonderful sensations of being in Shannon's hands and mouth. She was stroking him and licking him until he was fully erect. When she knew he was awake she slid her hands beneath his buttocks—as he had done to her—and lifted him, but instead of taking him into her mouth she aimed lower, and began licking his testicles and underneath his testicles. She avidly worked on him, wetting him, licking him dry, wetting him again, and then worked her way up the shaft of his thick penis until she reached the spongy head. Once there she licked all around it, took just the head into her mouth, wetting it thoroughly, and then finally engulfed his entire length. The sensation was so good that he lifted his butt off the bed and caught his breath. He felt her throat contracting on him, felt as if she were squeezing him again and again, milking him that way until he was almost ready to explode and then—as if sensing this—releasing him.

His penis came out glistening with her saliva. She used one hand to stroke him while the other fondled his balls, stroking, tickling them with her long, graceful fingers.

"Come up here," he said, reaching for her.

"Oh no," she said, pushing his hands away, "this time it's all about you. Just lie there and enjoy."

He didn't have to be told twice. Clint enjoyed giving pleasure to women, but the by-product of that act was that women wanted to give it back. If most men knew this, he was sure they'd treat women—their sweethearts, wives, even whores—a lot better.

She went back to work on him, using her hands, her mouth, her tongue and, at times, her teeth. She would bring him to the brink of orgasm and then skillfully hold off, only to once again take him to those heights. He'd never before had a woman do that to him, take him up and down like that, until he was at the point where he needed the release so bad he thought his entire body would explode.

She sensed this and, at that point, climbed up on top of him, took hold of him and guided him into her steamy depths. She began to ride him that way, slowly at first, and then faster. It may have been about him but that didn't mean she couldn't enjoy it, too. Soon they were both moaning and crying out and—as his release overcame him—Clint lifted his butt off the bed, taking her weight with him as his body went as taut as a bow and then . . . suddenly . . . let go . . .

Carl Breckens took himself back to the doorway across from the hotel where Clint Adams and George Markstein were staying. He was sharing a room with Aaron Edwards, and did not want to go back and listen to his partner snore. There was no way he'd get any thinking done that way.

He settled into the dark doorway, seating himself, and stared at the hotel. What were the chances, he wondered, of sneaking up there and killing Markstein tonight? Probably not good. After what had happened earlier in the day, even the desk clerk would have a heightened sense of alertness. And Markstein's room was down the hall from Clint Adams's. Breckens knew that the red-haired saloon girl had gone to his room with him, so the chances that he'd be asleep were slim. Breckens knew that if he had a girl like that in his room, he wouldn't get much sleep, either.

In fact, the local whorehouse did have a redhead. Not one that looked like the one from the saloon, but she was long and lean, the way Breckens liked his women, and she had a talented mouth.

A bed at the whorehouse, with that redhead, sure sounded better than sitting in this dark doorway. And he had the money to pay for the whole night. So after he was done with the whore, he could relax and give the situation all the thought it deserved.

He only had to weigh the two options for a few seconds before quitting the doorway and heading for the redhead and the bed.

# TWELVE

Clint woke the next morning with Shannon's weight on his right arm. It annoyed him, not because she was there, but because he had allowed her to fall asleep with his gun hand pinned beneath her. If someone had broken into the room with bad intentions, he'd be dead. As it was, the arm was numb when he pulled it from beneath her without waking her. He spent the next few minutes flexing and unflexing the hand and gritting his teeth against the pins-and-needles feeling that was shooting through it.

He sat up and swung his legs around, planting his bare feet on the wooden floor. He didn't know what Shannon had planned for the day, but all he had was supper with George Markstein to talk about the man's "business," and probably field a proposition for employment. If the man was looking to hire his gun, he was going to be out of luck.

He thought about waking Shannon, but she was a hard-working girl and could use her sleep. That was obvious from how soundly she was still sleeping. And if he woke her and they had sex one more time, he was sure that his penis would simply fall off. He was just happy he was able to stay with her as long as he had.

He stood up, got dressed and strapped on his gun belt.

Breakfast was the first order of the day—finding a place
that had a good one, and then consuming it. And coffee,
lots of hot, black, strong coffee.

He looked at Shannon O'Doyle once again. The sheet
had slipped down and was only covering her legs and half
of her butt, which was really a pretty fetching pose. He had
to talk himself out of getting back into bed with her, and
forced himself to walk out the door.

He asked the desk clerk to recommend a place for breakfast and then followed the man's directions to a busy
restaurant down the street. It was housed in a fairly new
building with big plateglass windows in front with the
name Hopper House emblazoned on the glass.

"Best food in town," the clerk had assured him. "Mr.
Hopper makes sure of that."

"He the cook?"

"The owner," the man said. "But he hires the cook. Tell
him we sent you over."

Clint assured the man he would do that.

As he entered, he was approached by a man in shirt-
sleeves and a string tie.

"Are you alone? I hope you're alone, because all I have
is a small table—"

Clint cut him off. "I'm alone."

"Ah, wonderful. Uh, it's in a corner, is that a problem?"

"I prefer a corner," Clint said, truthfully.

"Perfect! Come this way."

The man led him to a table that was exactly what he said
it was—small, and in a corner.

"Are you my waiter?" Clint asked.

"No, sir, I'm the owner," the man said. "My name is
Sam Hopper. I'll send your waiter right over, sir."

"Uh, thanks. I'm sorry, I meant no offense. I'm a
stranger in town."

"That's all right," the man said. "No offense taken. Can I start you with some coffee?"

"Yes, the blacker and stronger it is, the better."

"I'll have a pot made especially for you," Hopper said. "We have to treat our guests in town well."

"I appreciate that." Clint extended his hand. "My name's Clint Adams."

"Glad to know you, Mr. Adams," Hopper said, and went off to arrange for the coffee. But part of the way across the room he suddenly stopped and hunched his shoulders, then continued. Clint knew that he'd suddenly recognized the name.

He wasn't above using his name to make sure he got a good breakfast. After all, his name had to be good for something.

"Wake up!"

Aaron Edwards jerked awake, eyes wide, and stared at Carl Breckens, who was standing at the foot of his bed.

"What the—"

"Time to get up, damn it!" Breckens bellowed. "Why do I always have to shout in the morning to get your attention?"

Edwards rubbed his face vigorously, then looked at Breckens and said, "Huh?"

"Fuck it," Breckens said. "Just get dressed and meet me downstairs in the lobby."

Edwards looked over at Breckens's bed, which was still made and had not been slept in.

"What the—you were up all night, watching that hotel?"

Breckens almost told Edward that he'd spent the night in a whorehouse underneath a naked redhead, but then decided to let the man think what he liked.

"Somebody's got to do some work around here," he said.

Edwards stared at his partner. Damn, he already had his breakfast chaw in.

"Are you hearin' me, Aaron?" Breckens asked.

"Huh? Oh, yeah, right, down in the lobby."

"Ten minutes!" Breckens bellowed so it would penetrate the fog, and then left, slamming the door for good measure.

# THIRTEEN

Clint was in the middle of his breakfast when the sheriff walked into the place. He was greeted immediately by the owner, Hopper, who spoke rapidly and then pointed toward Clint. He wondered if, once the owner knew who Clint was, he'd actually sent for the lawman.

The longer he was in the restaurant, the more aware Clint had become that word had spread he was there. It had probably started in the kitchen and then, through the waiter, out to the patrons. Now, as Sheriff Cafferty walked toward him, all eyes were on him.

"You created quite a stir in here," the lawman said.

"A man's got to eat," Clint said, pointing with his knife at the steak and eggs. "Join me for coffee?"

"I'll join you for breakfast," Cafferty said, pulling out the other chair and seating himself. "I usually eat here anyway, and usually the same thing you're having."

"It's not bad," Clint admitted.

"Best in town."

The waiter, a young man in his late teens, came over and poured the sheriff some coffee. Clint noticed the boy's hand shaking while he was doing it.

"Did they send for you because I was eating here?"

"Well," the lawman said, lifting his cup, "in their defense they've never had a customer as famous as you before."

"Did they think I was going to shoot up the place?"

"They didn't know what to think," Cafferty said. He sipped his coffee and set it down. Clint was impressed the man did not comment on the strength of it. "I put their minds to rest."

"What did you tell them?"

"I said you were probably just hungry and not to worry."

"Good advice."

The waiter came back with the sheriff's plate.

"Can I get you anythin' else, Mr. Adams?" he asked.

"I'll let you know. What's your name, son?"

"My name? Uh, it's Willy . . . sir."

"Well, Willy, I'm not going to bite you or shoot you, so try and relax. Okay?"

"Oh, I'm not worried about that, sir," he said. "I'm just—you know—kinda excited that you're here and I get to wait on you."

"Well, try and keep your hands from shaking," Clint said. "We don't want any of our breakfast ending up in our laps, okay?"

"Yessir," the boy said. "I'll be careful."

"Good lad."

He went away and the sheriff cut into his steak.

"I want to thank you again for last night," Cafferty said. "If you hadn't acted when you did, I might have had to kill that card cheat."

"That's what I figured," Clint said. "Don't mention it."

They ate a few bites in silence and then the sheriff asked, "So what's goin' on with you and the man from the East? What's his name? Martin?"

"Markstein, and what do you mean?"

"I was making my rounds last night, saw the two of you cozying up in front of the hotel, smokin' cigars."

"You must not have been close enough. I wasn't smoking."

"No, I saw what you were intendin' to do, but it seems like he interrupted you."

"He wanted to go out for a walk. I suggested it wasn't a good idea. Then he said he wanted some air and a cigar, so I went out with him."

"He's got no idea what he's in for out here, does he?" the sheriff asked.

"Maybe not. After yesterday you'd think he would, though."

"What's he doin' in town? Did you ask?"

"No, but I'm supposed to have supper with him later," Clint said. "He's got something on his mind."

"Maybe he wants to hire your gun."

"I thought of that," Clint said, "and if that's the case, then he's plain out of luck."

"You don't hire out?" Cafferty asked.

"Never have, never will," Clint said. "I'm not a money gun, Sheriff. You've never heard that about me."

"You're right," the man said. "I haven't. Sorry I brought it up."

"That's okay."

They finished their breakfast and went outside after Clint paid his bill and noticed that the lawman never got one.

"So what are your plans for the day?" Cafferty asked.

"Keep myself occupied while I wait for supper," Clint said. "I'm kind of curious what the man has on his mind and why he's here."

"Well, if you find out anything you think I'd be interested in, let me know, will you?"

"Sure thing. Uh, what about those two cheats?"

"I thought about putting them in a cell overnight, but I put them on their horses and sent them on their way."

"In the dark, unarmed?"

"You don't approve."

"I approve wholeheartedly," Clint said. "I'm just wondering if they'd bother coming back."

"For their money? Or for their guns?"

"Both."

Cafferty shook his head.

"Didn't strike me as the type," he said. "I think they'll write it off and start over somewhere else."

"I hope you're right," Clint said. "If they come back, I'm thinking one of us might have to kill somebody."

"You already did that this week," Cafferty reminded him. "Take the rest of the week off, will ya?"

# FOURTEEN

Clint was waiting in the lobby when George Markstein came down from his room for supper.

"Ah, excellent," the easterner said. "I hope I didn't keep you waiting too long."

He was wearing a suit that would have fit in fine in New York or San Francisco, but for Kingman, Arizona, the man was clearly overdressed.

"No, I wasn't waiting long," Clint told him.

"Have you picked out a restaurant?"

"Yes," Clint said. "I had breakfast there and it was very good. It'll be busy, though."

"No problem," Markstein said. "As long as we get to eat. I'm starving."

They left the hotel and headed for Hopper House.

"What have you done with yourself today?" Markstein asked.

"Not much, just took a look around town."

"You've never been here before?"

"I've been around here, but never actually in Kingman," Clint said. "What about you? What did you do?"

"I took your advice and stayed inside."

"And out of trouble," Clint said. "That's good."

"Although I don't know if I'm going to be able to do that forever," Markstein said.

"Forever? Are you staying around here that long?"

"Well, perhaps not forever," Markstein said, "but I will be around here for some time."

"On business?"

"Precisely," Markstein said, "and that is the very thing I want to talk to you about."

"Your business?" Clint asked.

"Let's talk when we're seated and eating," Markstein said.

When they entered the restaurant, the owner, Hopper, came running over to them.

"Mr. Adams, how nice to see you back so soon," he said, shaking Clint's hand.

"Mr. Hopper," Clint said. "I wasn't sure you'd want me back."

"No, no," Hopper said, and then, "nononono, not at all. I only sent for the sheriff to—"

"That's okay, Mr. Hopper," Clint said, "don't worry about it. My friend and I would like to have supper."

"Of course, of course." Hopper looked around the crowded dining room. "How about the same table?"

"Perfect."

"It's small and not many of my customers like sitting in a corner," Hopper continued.

"Must we sit in a corner?" Markstein asked. "Why can't we have that table over—"

Clint put his hand on Markstein's arm and said to Hopper, "The corner table is fine."

"This way."

He seated them and promised to send over their waiter.

"Is it Willy?"

"Yes, he's still working."

"Good," Clint said. "Maybe he's calmer now and his hands won't shake so much."

"He's young," Hopper said, "and very impressed with you."

When Hopper left, Markstein said, "Impressed with you? You seem to be fairly well known for someone who just got to town. Should I, uh, know who you are?"

"No reason why you should," Clint said. "We don't travel in the same circles."

Markstein sat back and stared at Clint.

"You are being modest, I think," Markstein said. "I can ask your Mr. Hopper, or the sheriff."

"So you really don't know?" Clint asked, wondering if the man was just playing dumb.

"I really don't."

"I have a reputation with a gun," Clint said. "I'm called the Gunsmith."

Clint could see that name register with Markstein.

"Oh, my, yes," Markstein said. "I have heard of you by that name."

Clint didn't say anything.

"Oh, my, now I understand how you managed to save my life with such ease."

"There's nothing easy about killing a man, Mr. Markstein."

"No, no, of course not. I didn't mean—I'm sorry."

"Forget it."

Willy came over, and Markstein allowed Clint to order for both of them.

"Something everyone eats here in the West," Markstein said.

Clint ordered two steak dinners.

"Do you have beer?" Clint asked.

"Yessir," Willy said.

"Then two beers."

"Yessir."

"That young man is . . . frightened of you," Markstein said.

"He's just a little excited, that's all."

"It must be interesting."

"What?"

"Having everyone know you," the man said. "Perhaps fear you . . . or maybe respect you."

"All of those things happen," Clint said, "and, yes, it tends to make life interesting."

"I'm sure if that man you killed— What was his name? Dolan? I'm sure he would not have tried to shoot you if he knew who you were."

"Maybe not," Clint said. "You'd be surprised at how many men decide to shoot it out *because* they know who I am."

"Ah," Markstein said, nodding sagely, "man's ever present desire to test himself."

"Something like that."

"How does it feel to—"

"Can we change the subject now?" Clint said, cutting him off. "Didn't you have something you wanted to ask me?"

"I did, yes," Markstein said, "but since discovering who you are, I was thinking that perhaps you wouldn't be interested."

"What else have we got to do for the next couple of hours?" Clint asked. "Go ahead and try me."

# FIFTEEN

"Do you know what this is?"

Markstein took something from his pocket and put it on the table between them.

"It's a blue rock with some brown veins running through it," Clint said without touching it.

"Yes, it is, but it has a name," Markstein said. "It's turquoise."

"That's turquoise?" Clint asked. "I've seen turquoise before, and that doesn't look anything like it."

"This is a piece of rough turquoise," Markstein explained. He picked it up. "I found it in Philadelphia, bought it, and managed to track it down to one of the mines in this region."

"Then what happened?"

Markstein put the stone back in his pocket.

"I bought the mine."

"And that's why you're here?" Clint asked. "To work the mine?"

"To oversee the working of the mine, yes," Markstein said. "It is one of the largest mines in the area and is already being worked quite successfully."

"How did you get to buy it, then?" Clint asked. "I mean, why did the original owner want to sell it?"

"I made a lump sum offer and he took it," Markstein said. "That was more preferable to him than digging the stones out and eventually turning them into cash for himself."

"So you're going to your mine from here?"

"Yes."

"Where is it?"

"Near someplace called Beale Springs."

"I don't know it."

"You wouldn't," Markstein said. "I understand it's very small and used to be a water stop. At one time it was called Fort Beale Springs, but the military has left it long behind."

"When were you planning on heading out?"

"Well, as soon as I could find a guide."

"You'll have to be careful about that," Clint said. "You're likely to find yourself being guided right into an ambush."

"Ah, and so we come to my offer."

"I can't guide you, George," Clint said, trying to head the man off. "Like I said, I don't know the area all that well."

"I realize that," Markstein said. "I was hoping that you would help me find a guide. You are much wiser in the ways of the West than I could ever hope to be."

Clint couldn't argue with that.

"I suppose I could do that," he said. "Shouldn't take me very long and then we can be on our separate ways."

"Well, no, that's not all of my offer," Markstein said as Willy arrived with their plates. They both sat back to allow him to set them down. He had brought their beers earlier.

"What do you mean?" Clint asked.

"I would like you to come to the mine with me," Markstein said.

"Why?"

"Because I know nothing about mining."

"You said there are people in place," Clint said. "I don't know much about mining, either—turquoise mining, anyway."

"But you've done some."

"I was involved in a gold mine for a while, but—"

"It should be about the same thing," Markstein said, "but still, that's not it either."

"Then what is it?"

"I don't know what kind of reception I'm going to get up there," Markstein said, finally.

"What do you mean?"

"Well, when I said I bought the mine I meant I bought half of it."

"Oh, I see."

"Yes, the other partner would not sell. So, I have a partner, and not a willing one."

"So you want . . . what? A bodyguard?"

"I want someone who will look out for my interests," Markstein said. "Someone at home with this part of the country and with the people. And the fact that you are who you are . . . well, that's just a bonus."

Clint believed him, because Markstein had told him about his offer before he found out who Clint was.

"If you are on your way somewhere, then I won't bother you," Markstein said. "If, however, you have no one waiting for you at the moment, I would offer you whatever payment you require. Perhaps a small piece of the mine?"

"No," Clint said. "That won't be necessary. Like I said, I've had some experience with gold mines and I don't really want to be an owner again."

"Then payment?"

Clint chewed a piece of excellently prepared meat while he gave it some thought.

"Sure, why not?" he said after he'd swallowed.

"How much?"

"Whatever you think is fair," Clint said. "I have to admit I'll be doing this out of curiosity, not for the money."

"Excellent!" Markstein said happily. "I will make it worth your while, I assure you."

"I believe you, George," Clint said, "but how about we set that aside for now and get down to eating these steaks?"

"I agree wholeheartedly."

# SIXTEEN

They did not discuss business any further over dinner, but did come back to it during dessert. Once again George Markstein offered Clint a small piece of the mine for his help.

"I owe you a partial partnership just for saving my life yesterday," the man insisted.

"George, I appreciate it," Clint said, "but I don't want to be a mine owner. I'll find us a guide and ride up there with you to look the operation over and see what kind of a reception you get. That's all."

"That is hardly all, Clint," Markstein said. "That is quite a bit."

When they finished eating, Markstein insisted on paying the bill.

"It will be the first installment of what I will be paying you," Markstein said. "In fact, I will be paying all your expenses from now on, including your hotel."

"Well, we'll have plenty of other expenses."

"Such as?"

"You'll need a horse, we'll need a packhorse and supplies for the ride to the mine," Clint explained. "We can look for all that stuff tomorrow, while I'm looking for a guide."

"And how will you find someone you can trust?" Markstein asked.

"Simple," Clint said. "I'll ask somebody I trust."

Clint found Sheriff Cafferty in his office, going through wanted posters and flyers.

"If you're looking for me, I'm not in there," Clint said.

"Not lookin' for anyone in particular," the lawman said, setting them aside. "What can I do for you?"

"I need a guide," Clint said.

"To go where?"

"Up into the mountains, somewhere above Beale Springs."

"To a mine?"

"Yep."

"I didn't know you had any interest in the mines."

"Neither did I, until tonight."

The sheriff sat back in his chair.

"Ah, I see. You had your supper with Mr. Markstein."

"He's got a piece of a mine," Clint said. "That's what he's doing here."

"And he wants you to go with him to find it?"

Clint explained Markstein's offer to the sheriff, so that the lawman would know exactly what was going on.

"I get it," he said. "Lemme think. Somebody you can trust. That's not easy to come by in a mining town. Somebody's always looking to get somethin' for nothin'."

"I figured if anyone would know somebody, it'd be you."

"Uh-huh." The lawman rubbed his jaw. "You payin'?"

"Markstein's paying, but yeah, we're paying."

"You want somebody who can use a gun?"

"Give me somebody well-rounded," Clint said. "Somebody I can just tell what I want, and get it."

"Well, there's Bill Cryder, but he usually has to be told specifically what to do, step by step."

"Save him for the end. Who else?"

"There's James Washburn," Cafferty said. "He might do, but the funny thing is, he don't ride very good. Tends to fall off horses a lot."

"Anybody else?"

"Yeah, I think so," Cafferty said. "There's a new feller in town. Now, I don't know him that well, but he's been around for a few months doin' odd jobs, and I never heard anybody complain about him."

"Does he know his way around?"

"Oh yeah, he's guided some supply wagons up the mountain."

"He sounds like the likely candidate, then," Clint said. "What's his name and where would I find him?"

# SEVENTEEN

The sheriff told Clint he'd find his guide in a saloon called Saloon No. 1. He explained that this was the first saloon to open in Kingman. He also explained that this was not a good part of town to loiter in, but his man seemed to be most comfortable there.

"He's a loner," Cafferty said. "Does most of his work on his own. Doesn't have any friends that I can see."

"Well, I don't want to be his friend," Clint said. "I just need a guide."

Clint entered Saloon No. 1 and saw what Cafferty had been talking about. It was a ramshackle building that looked as if it was about to fall down, and it didn't improve when you went inside. The bar looked to be leaning to one side, which probably made it easier to slide beer mugs downhill. The tables and chairs were mismatched, and many of them were either three- or three-and-a-half legged.

He walked up to the bar and had no trouble getting the bartender's attention since he was already the center of it.

"What can I get ya?"

"Some information."

"Fresh out." The man had bulging biceps, but also a bulging belly.

"I haven't asked you anything, yet."

"It don't matter."

"Okay," Clint said, "before we get off on the wrong foot, I'm looking for a man to give him a job."

The bartender relaxed and replied, "Shoulda said that from the beginning. Who's the guy?"

"Goes by the name Buck Chance." It sounded like an alias to Clint, but who was he to judge. Maybe the reason the man stayed to himself was because he was running from something. That didn't matter to Clint, either.

"Sittin' in the back, alone," the bartender said. "Starin' into his beer."

"Thanks."

"You want somethin' now?"

"Sure," Clint said. "Give me a beer."

The bartender drew him one and slid it downhill to him. When Clint caught it, he realized why Chance might be staring into his. It was to check and see what was floating in it.

Clint nodded at the bartender, picked up the mug and carried it back to Buck Chance's table.

"Mind if I sit?" he asked.

"Why would you want to?" Chance asked without looking up.

"I might have a job for you."

Now the man looked up. Clint was startled by the blue of his eyes. He'd never seen eyes that blue on a man.

"In that case you better sit down, Mr. Adams."

Clint sat and said, "You know who I am."

"You sort of announced your presence in town when you gunned down Mike Dolan."

"Friend of yours?"

"I don't have any friends in Kingman," Chance said. "Whoever sent you to me musta told you that."

"Sheriff Cafferty," Clint said. "He sent me."

"Fact is," Chance added, "a few more days or weeks I mighta had to gun Dolan myself."

"Why's that?"

Chance shrugged.

"Boredom," he said, then added, "plus Mike deserved it."

"That's what I've heard."

"And what've you heard about me?"

"That you're for hire," Clint said, "that you usually work alone, and that so far, you're trustworthy."

Chance smiled and said, "That's only because I haven't cheated anyone . . . yet."

"You planning on it?"

"Not plannin'," Chance said, "but you never know."

Clint thought he detected an accent in the man's speech—southern maybe, or more specifically—

"Louisiana?" Clint asked.

"What?"

"I'm thinkin' maybe New Orleans," Clint went on. "Or maybe . . . Baton Rouge?"

Chance sat back and stared across the table.

"That's good," he said. "It's Baton Rouge. You know what my real last name is?"

"Not if you don't want me to."

"Oh, I ain't wanted or anything," Chance said. "I just didn't want to travel through the West tellin' folks my last name was Bon Chance."

"Ouch."

"Yeah," he said, "and my real first name ain't Buck, either, but I ain't tellin' that one."

"Well, your secret's safe with me."

"What's the job?"

"Guide."

"Where?"

"One of the mines above Beale Springs."

"One of the big ones?"

"Yes."

"Which one?"

That stumped Clint.

"I don't know the name of it, but I've got an easterner here in town who bought into it and wants to check it out."

"That must be the Blue Lady Mine," Chance said, with a smile. "I heard one of the partners sold out. When do you want to go?"

"Tomorrow morning. I thought we'd use today to stock up on supplies, get a packhorse, and my man needs a horse, as well.

"You hirin' me for tomorrow, or right now?"

"Right now."

"Your guy got money?"

"He bought a mine, didn't he?"

"Good point." Chance named a figure and pushed his chair back. "That gonna buckle his knees?"

"I doubt it."

"Then I'd say you fellas got yourself a guide." He stood and put out his hand. He was a little over six feet, a fit-looking thirty or so. Clint shook his hand and took a look at the man's gun and holster. They were well cared for, and worn like he knew how to use them.

"Let's go," Chance said.

"Don't you want to finish your beer?"

"Are you kiddin'?" Chance asked. "Did you look in your mug yet?"

Clint glanced at the trio of flies floating in there and said, "I see what you mean."

As they headed for the door, Chance said, "Since you just hired me, you wanna pay my tab?"

# EIGHTEEN

Since Kingman was only two or three years removed from having been a one-horse town, it didn't take long for Breckens and Edwards to locate Clint Adams after they missed him at the hotel that morning.

"If you'd get your ass outta bed the first time I call ya—" Breckens was still complaining to Edwards.

"Okay, okay, I get it, it's my fault we missed him at the hotel," Edwards said. "Can we let it drop now?"

They dropped it, but Breckens kept muttering to himself until they saw Clint Adams walking up Beale Street with another man. Breckens pushed Edwards into a doorway.

"Who the hell is that?" Breckens demanded.

"You know who that is, Carl," Edward said. "He drinks at Number One all the time. It's that fella Chance."

"Crap," Breckens said.

"They probably just hired him to guide them to the mine," Edwards said. "What's the big deal?"

"It's another man we might have to kill," Breckens said. "We've gone from one to three now, and all for the same money."

Breckens never told his partner that he'd gotten some money from their employer already.

"Well, we don't even know for sure that the dandy hired Adams, yet," Edwards said. "If he did, then we're gonna need help."

"Great," Breckens said, "more fingers in the pie."

"Are we havin' pie?"

"Shut up."

Clint took Chance to the hotel first to meet the man who was going to be paying all the bills. George Markstein opened the door to his room and invited them in.

"I'm pleased to make your acquaintance, Mr. Chance," he said after Clint had made the introductions, "and very pleased that you'll be guiding us to our destination."

"I hope you're still pleased after you hear what you've got to pay me," Chance said.

Markstein looked at Clint, and then back at Chance.

"And how much is that?"

Chance told him and waited for his knees to buckle.

"That's not a problem," Markstein said without flinching.

"Good," Chance said. "Then we're all set."

"Is there something I should be doing?" Markstein asked.

"No," Chance said, "you've hired me, so the rest is my job. If you'll give me some money, I'll go and buy some supplies."

"I'll go and buy the horses," Clint said.

"Wait," Markstein said. He walked over to his suitcase and took out a wallet. From it he extracted a bunch of bills and brought them back to Chance and Clint.

"How much will you need?"

Clint plucked some bills from the man's hands and said, "This should do it for the horses. If I can, I'll just rent them. That'll be cheaper."

"And we'll only have to camp one night," Chance said, taking some bills, "so this should be plenty."

Markstein seemed surprised that he still had some of the money left in his hands.

"You look surprised," Clint said. "Did you think we'd take all the money?"

"I think I might have been fortunate enough to find two honest men in Kingman," Markstein said.

"Don't be so sure about me," Chance said. He turned to Clint. "I'll pick up the supplies and meet you at the livery."

"Fine," Clint said. "It'll take me a while to pick out a couple of likely horses."

They left the hotel together and stopped briefly out in front.

"We have some rough terrain to cover," Chance said, "unless we just stick to the roads, which I would do if I was guiding somebody with wagons."

"Well, we're not in a hurry," Clint said, "but one night on the trail should be enough."

"Okay, then," Chance said, "pick out a couple of sure-footed horses. See if they have any buckskins; they generally have harder hooves."

"I'll do my best," Clint said.

"You ride that Darley Arabian, don't you?" Chance asked.

"That's right."

"Then I guess you won't have any trouble pickin' out horses. I shouldn't be tellin' you what to look for."

"No problem," Clint said. "The more I know about what our ride's going to be like, the better choices I can make."

"On the other hand," Chance said, "we just might have to settle for what we can get."

"We'll just have to wait and see."

They split up there, Chance heading for the mercantile and Clint for the livery.

"Let's take Adams now," Edwards said as they watched the two men go their own ways.

"You know, for the first time in your life you said somethin' smart a minute ago," Breckens said.

"I did?" Edwards looked puzzled. "What was it?"

"That we don't know if the dandy's even hired Clint Adams," Breckens said. "Until we do know that, why would we chance goin' up against him?"

"Okay, then how do we find out?"

"We just keep watchin'," Breckens said, "and waitin'."

# NINETEEN

When Clint had first left Eclipse at the livery, he'd only concerned himself with the liveryman's ability to take care of his horse. Now, as he entered, he took a better look at the overall operation. The place looked well cared for, and the horses stabled there looked healthy, which was important. Too many times he'd seen mangy horses in liveries, and had refused to board his own horse there, whether it was Duke in the old days, or Eclipse now.

"Back to check on your big boy?" the liveryman asked. He approached, wiping his scarred hands on a rag. He was in his sixties and bore all the earmarks of a man who had handled horses all his life—including parts of two fingers missing, having been bitten off. "He's doin' real good."

"Actually, I need a couple of horses for a trek up to one of the mines," Clint said.

"Saddle horses?"

"One saddle, one pack animal."

"Actually," the man said, "I've got two for you that will do the trick, for sure. They're out back."

"Let's go have a look."

The man led Clint through the stable to a back door and along the way said, "My name's Axel."

"Clint Adams."

"I know," Axel said. "It's a real honor to have your horse in my place, Mr. Adams."

"Thanks."

Out back was a corral with about a dozen horses in it.

"You lookin' ta buy or just rent?"

"I think it would make more sense for me to rent them," Clint said. "We'll be comin' back this way and I can return them with no problem."

"Okay," Axel said. "I got two buckskins in here the other day that I think will do the job. You know why?"

"Because their hooves are harder than most horses'?"

Axel cackled and said, "I knew you was a man who knew horses."

Clint wasn't sure he even knew that about buckskins until Buck Chance had told him. He wondered if Chance's knowledge of buckskins had anything to do with the fact that he'd chosen the name Buck to replace his real name.

"See them two, in the back?" Axel said. "One's a golden hair, one's a dun, but they're both buckskins."

"Let me have a closer look."

They approached the corral and the man opened the gate so they could enter, then closed it behind them.

As they walked through the corral, the horses scattered to let them through. When they reached the two buckskins, Axel stood aside proudly and allowed Clint to examine them. Clint concerned himself mostly with the condition of their legs, which seemed sturdy enough.

He placed his hand on the haunches of the golden-haired mare and asked, "This one is, what, six?"

"Yep."

"And the dun gelding? Four?"

"Five, just turned."

They were good-sized horses, the mare actually bigger than the gelding—sixteen hands to slightly over fifteen.

"Whataya think?"

"I think we should go inside and talk price," Clint said.

"I got me a bottle of good whiskey we can do it over," Axel said anxiously.

"I hope you're not one of those fellas who likes dickering," Clint said as they walked back through the corral.

"Well, now—"

"Because I hate dickering," Clint said. "I like a man who sets a fair price the first time through."

"Well," Axel said, as they reentered the livery, "that don't make for much whiskey drinkin', does it?"

"Well," Clint said, slapping the older man on the back, "certainly not a whole bottle."

# TWENTY

By the time Buck Chance found his way to the livery, Clint and Axel had come to terms on renting the two horses.

"I know you," Axel said as Chance entered. "I got your sorrel in number four."

"That's right." He looked at Clint. "How'd we do?"

"Like you said," Clint replied. "Two buckskins. How'd you know."

"I saw one over here the other day," Chance said. "I was just hoping he had two."

"You want them ready to go in the mornin'?" Axel asked.

"Oh, hell," Clint said, "I forgot about a saddle."

"I got one," Axel said. "Ain't great, but it'll do. Fella couldn't pay his bill last month, so I took his saddle."

"Let's see it," Chance said.

Axel went and brought the saddle back with him. It was worn, but like he had said, it would do.

"Throw it in," Clint said.

"Wha— Aw, okay," Axel said. "What the hell, I ain't never gonna sell it, and this way I'll get it back . . . right?"

"Right," Clint said.

"Is our employer a horseman?" Chance asked.

"You know, that's something I never asked him," Clint said. "But he won't squawk either way."

"I'm havin' the supplies delivered here early tomorrow," Chance told Clint and Axel.

"I'll pack yer horse, if you want," Axel offered. "No extra charge."

"You remember which one to pack and which one to saddle, you can do both," Clint said.

"I'll remember."

"Good man." He looked at Chance. "I guess we're set."

"I hate to bring it up," Chance said, "but does our man have a gun? A rifle?"

"I'll find out."

"You don't know much about him, do you?"

"I've seen the color of his money."

"Good point. How about some lunch?"

"Sounds good. I've got some money left."

"So do I. Hopper House?"

"Why not?" Clint asked. "Been eating there since I got to town."

"Found the best place right off, huh?" Chance said. "Me, I ain't eaten there in awhile. Be nice to get some good food into my belly."

"Sounds good," Axel said, eyeing them both.

"Oh, hell, Axel," Clint said, "why don't you come along?"

"Really?" the liveryman said. "I ain't never et at Hopper House."

"Go get cleaned up some," Clint said. "We'll wait."

"Cleaned up?" the man said, aghast. "You don't mean . . . a bath?"

"Just get some of the horse smell off of you," Clint said. "We don't want to get kicked out before we have a chance to eat."

"I got me some bay rum in the back," Axel said. "You know, case I ever meet a lady?"

"Well, wash yourself off in that horse trough back there and then slap on some bay rum. We'll wait out front."

"I'll hurry it up!" he said anxiously. "Don't leave without me."

Clint and Chance went out in front of the livery to wait.

"You know you're bein' followed," Chance said to Clint.

"I know," Clint said. "Spotted them right off. Two men. Sometimes they take turns, sometimes both."

"What's it about?"

"Don't know," Clint said. "Might be friends of Mike Dolan."

"Way I heard it, Dolan didn't have no friends."

"You mean like you?"

"No," Chance said. "I got no friends because I don't want 'em. Dolan didn't have no friends because he was a sonofabitch."

"I got you," Clint said. "In any case, I've just sort of been waiting on them to make some kind of move."

"I end up gettin' shot, I'm gonna want some hazard pay," Chance told him.

"I think I can get Markstein to go for that," Clint said.

Axel appeared from around the side of the stable, running. The smell of bay rum preceded him.

"Thought you mighta left without me," he said. "We ready to strap on that feed bag?"

"The question is," Clint said, "are they ready for us?"

"I don't like it," Breckens said.

"Like what? That they're eatin' and we're not?"

"Chance went and bought supplies, enough for an overnight to one of the mines," Breckens said. "That means he's probably gonna guide the dandy to his mine."

"And Adams?"

"He was lookin' at horses, and if you've seen his horse you know he don't need one."

"So?"

"So all that means that the three of them are gonna be headin' up the mountain tomorrow."

"So we need help?"

Breckens, going against everything in him, said, "Yeah, we need help."

# TWENTY-ONE

Hopper was appalled when Clint and Chance entered his restaurant with Axel—even more so because he had to give them a table in the middle of the room, because they would not all fit at the corner table Clint had used earlier.

Clint wasn't comfortable with the center table, so he was going to have to keep an even warier eye out while he ate.

"I'll watch your back," Chance promised him.

"Thanks."

As it turned out, Axel wasn't embarrassing at all. He ate slowly, and carefully, and did not use his hands. This seemed to mollify the owner somewhat.

They all had bowls of beef stew, soaked it all up with biscuits and washed it down with beer.

"I gotta thank you fellers," Axel said. "I ain't et that good in years." He stood up. "I'll be sure to have your horses and supplies ready in the mornin'. Six a.m.?"

"Six is fine," Chance said.

Axel left and Clint and Chance ordered pie and coffee.

"You got a rifle to go with that handgun?" Clint asked Chance.

"Sure," the other man said. "I got a knife and a saddle, too. And an extra shirt."

"Okay, okay," Clint said, in the face of the man's sarcasm, "I was just asking."

"Yeah, okay," Chance said. "Just figure that you hired me because I know what I'm doin', okay?"

"Okay."

After lunch Chance said he had to go take care of some personal stuff so he'd be ready to leave in the morning. Clint said he'd meet him in front of the livery at six a.m.

"You need any more spending money?" Clint asked.

"No, I'm good," Chance said. "I'll see you in the morning."

Clint watched as Chance went up the street. The two men who thought they were so adept at trailing somebody did not bother to follow him. They stayed with Clint. He considered crossing the street and asking them point blank what was on their minds, but he knew the sheriff wouldn't take kindly to him killing anyone else while he was in town. If these two men were trying to get up the nerve to confront him, they would have done it by now. If he went and braced them, he might force them into action.

He decided to go back to the hotel and report to George Markstein on everything they had done.

"Sounds very impressive for a day's work," Markstein said.

"So, you'll be ready in the morning?" Clint asked. "Before first light?"

"I am normally an early riser, Mr. Adams," Markstein said. "I will be more than ready."

"And how's your head?"

Markstein touched his bandage. "I have a headache, but the doctor assures me it will be gone soon," the easterner said.

"I need to ask you a few things, George."

"Ask away." Markstein was sitting on his bed, in shirt-sleeves and trousers. He placed his hands on his knees and waited.

"Can you use a gun?" Clint asked.

"A handgun or a rifle?"

"Either one?"

"I am an expert marksman with a rifle," Markstein said proudly. "My skill with a handgun is not so good."

"Your expertise with a rifle," Clint said. "Target shooting?"

"Yes," the other man said. "Trap shooting, skeet shooting, some deer hunting."

"You've never killed a man?"

"Heavens, no."

"Never fired at a man?"

"No."

"Do you think you could ever fire at a man?"

"Well . . . if it was self-defense, I suppose . . ."

"Don't suppose, George," Clint said. "If you don't think you can do it, let me know now."

The man thought about it for a moment and said, "Well, I guess . . . no, I know, if our lives were in danger, I would . . . shoot at a man."

"Shoot to kill?"

"Yes," Markstein said, squaring his shoulders, "shoot to kill. Do you think we may . . . have to do that?"

"There have been two men following us," Clint said, "following me, actually."

"What do they want?"

"I don't know," Clint said. "They may be harmless."

"What if it's not you they're after?" Markstein asked. "What if it's me? And my mine?"

"It could be," Clint said. "If it is, they'll probably follow us up there."

"And that is where we may have to defend ourselves?"

Markstein asked. "That's why you've been asking me if I'd shoot a man?"

"Yes."

"Well then," Markstein said, "if they are after my mine, the answer is definitely yes. I would kill to protect my mine."

"Okay," Clint said, "that's what I wanted to know."

# TWENTY-TWO

After leaving the hotel, Clint entered Sheriff Cafferty's office and found it empty. He'd never encountered a deputy, and didn't find one now. He looked back in the cell block and found only empty cells. He was about to leave when the front door opened and the sheriff stepped in.

"Adams," the man said. "To what do I owe the pleasure?"

"Just wanted to check in with you on a couple of things," Clint said.

"Can you do it while I make a pot of coffee?" Cafferty asked, walking to the cast-iron stove that looked as if it had once been in somebody's kitchen.

"I don't see why not."

"Wait, I've got to get some water." He grabbed a pot and went out a back door, leaving it open. Clint heard the sound of a pump, and then Cafferty came back in, closing the door behind him. He grabbed a handful of grounds and dropped them into the pot, then lit the stove and set the pot on top.

"Let's sit," he said, and went around behind his desk. "What's on your mind?"

"Two things," Clint said, seating himself. "I hired Buck Chance and he's going to guide us to the Blue Lady Mine."

"The Blue Lady? That's your friend's mine?"

"Apparently. Why?"

He thought Cafferty was smirking, but it disappeared and he couldn't be sure.

"No reason. When are you leavin'?"

"First light."

"You'll spend one night on the trail, then."

"That's what we figured."

"Chance'll do right by you."

"I think so, too," Clint said.

"What was the other thing?"

"I've got two idiots following me around."

"How do you know they're idiots?"

"Well, first, they're following me around."

"Good point."

"Second, they think I don't see them."

"Maybe they're fans," the sheriff said.

"And maybe not," Clint said. "If something goes wrong, I want you to know I tried to avoid it."

"You think they're gonna try you?"

"I don't know," Clint said. "If they were going to, they probably would have done it by now."

"Then what?" Cafferty asked. "You think it's got somethin' to do with your friend's mine?"

"Well, I didn't," Clint said, "but now I do, maybe."

"Describe them."

Clint did, in detail, and Cafferty listened intently, then started shaking his head.

"Don't know them?" Clint asked.

"The opposite," Cafferty said. "I know a dozen of 'em."

"I was afraid of that."

"Do you want me to watch your back, grab 'em and question 'em?" the lawman asked.

"No," Clint said, standing up, "I'll handle it."

"Not by killin' them, I hope."

"Not unless they force me into it," Clint said. "Besides, if it happens on the trail, or up at the mine—"

"I'm the sheriff for all of Mohave County, Adams," Cafferty said. "If somethin' happens at one of the mines, they send for me."

"How do you do these jobs without deputies?"

"I've had deputies," the lawman said. "Like the men following you, most of them have been idiots, not worth the effort it took to pin a badge on them."

"Too bad," Clint said. "Sounds like you could use some help."

"You volunteering?"

"Not me," Clint said. "I've got a job."

"I could pay you twenty dollars a month."

"Tempting, but no."

Clint headed for the door.

"Adams."

"Yeah?"

"Do me a favor."

"What?"

"You have to kill them two jaspers on the trail?" Cafferty said. "Bury 'em there."

"I'll keep that in mind."

Carl Breckens regarded the two men sitting across from him at Saloon No. 1. Aaron Edwards wasn't there; he was still keeping an eye on Clint Adams.

"Have you both got this straight?" he asked.

"Yeah, sure," one of them, Jeff Kemp, said. "We got three men to kill."

"One is more important than the other two," Breckens said. "The other two we only kill if we have to, if they get in the way."

"We got it," Kemp's partner, Paul Drake, said.

"And nobody fires until I say so."

"We got it, Carl," Kemp said. "When do we do this?"

"They're headin' out tomorrow," Breckens said. "We'll hit them somewhere on the trail. They can't get to that mine. Understand?"

"We understand, Carl," Kemp said. "We ain't stupid."

"Just make sure we get paid what we agreed on," Drake said.

"Don't worry," Breckens said, "this job gets done, we all get paid."

# TWENTY-THREE

Clint was hungry for supper after the big lunch he had with Buck Chance and Axel. Since he didn't know what he'd find in Beale Springs, or at the Blue Lady Mine, he decided to indulge some of his vices again that night. He went to the Nighthawk Saloon and saw Shannon working the floor. She spotted him when he walked in and waved but did not abandon the men whose table she was sitting at.

He walked to the crowded bar, elbowed himself a spot and waved down the bartender.

"Back for more?" the man asked. "Don't think there's a game goin' in this crowd."

"That's okay," Clint said. "I'll just take a beer."

"Comin' up."

The other men at the bar seemed to recognize him, because they had cleared out more room for him than he actually needed. Clint didn't mind. He liked the extra room.

The bartender came with Clint's beer, took his money and went down to the other end. Clint turned and watched Shannon talk to three men at a table. She was sitting on the lap of one of them, doing her job, keeping them happy and drinking. He knew she was very good at her job, and he knew she was even better at her job when it wasn't a job.

Eventually she left the lap of the man, stroked his face with her hand, went by a couple of other tables and made her way over to Clint.

"It's hard to work tonight," she told him, coming in close so he could smell her and look down her dress. "My legs are still shaking."

"Mine, too," he said. "I think you were trying to kill me."

"Me?" she said. "I could hardly keep up with you. What brings you here tonight? I'm sure it's not the beer."

"I have to leave in the morning."

She looked surprised.

"For good?"

"No," he said. "I'm going up to one of the mines. I'm sure I'll be back in a couple of days."

"Which mine?"

"The Blue Lady," he said. "This fellow I know bought a piece of it and a man named Buck Chance and I are taking him up there."

"The Blue Lady?" she asked, taking a step back.

"That's right."

"And you think you'll be back in a few days?" she demanded.

"Four or five at the most."

"You think I'm gonna believe that, Clint Adams?"

"Shannon . . . what are you talking about?"

"Yeah, like you don't know."

"I really don't—"

"Right," she said. "Look, I've got work to do. You enjoy your visit to the Blue Lady Mine."

"Shannon," he said, but she stormed off, leaving him very confused.

He returned to his hotel and figured since he was alone he might as well just go to bed. He was going to need a good night's sleep in order to make that early start, anyway.

What the hell was wrong with people when they found out he was going to the Blue Lady Mine? he wondered as he got between the sheets. There was something about this mine that made Shannon mad and put a smirk on the face of the sheriff. Were they going to find something up there that was not going to make George Markstein happy? More than once a man had been swindled by buying a mine sight unseen. Maybe that was going to happen this time.

Clint realized there were still too many questions he hadn't asked George Markstein. He resolved to get to those in the morning before they started their trek to Beale Springs and up the mountain to the Blue Lady turquoise mine.

If there was anything fishy about this deal, he wanted to know before he got in the saddle.

# TWENTY-FOUR

When he knocked on George Markstein's door, he was surprised to find it opened right away by a wide-awake man.

"Good morning, good morning," Markstein said cheerfully. "Are we ready to go?"

"We are," Clint said, "but I've got a question or two I need answered before we go any further, George."

"Ask, then," Markstein said. "I have nothing to hide from the man who saved my life."

"You bought this mine sight unseen?"

"That's right."

"But on the word of someone?"

"Yes, indeed," Markstein said, "someone I trust implicitly."

"So there's nothing funny going on at this mine that you know about?" Clint asked.

"No, sir," Markstein said, and then added, "why, have you heard something?"

"It's just that people are looking at me funny when I say I'm going up to the Blue Lady Mine."

"I swear," Markstein said, "I don't know why."

"Okay," Clint said, "I guess we'll find out when we get there."

As they started down the hall, Clint suddenly thought of something. He put his hand out to stop their progress.

"I have one more question, which I should have asked earlier," he said.

"And what's that?"

"You can ride, can't you?"

"Oh, yes," Markstein said, "I am quite an accomplished rider."

Clint breathed a sigh of relief that they weren't going to have to spend the morning finding and renting a buckboard.

Buck Chance was waiting outside the livery stable with Axel, with their horses saddled and the packhorse loaded.

"Right on time," Chance said.

"Good morning, Mr. Chance," Markstein said.

"This is Axel," Clint said.

"He's been very helpful," Chance informed them.

"Axel." At that point Markstein started to look around. "What about the man following us—"

"Don't look around like that!" Clint snapped.

"Sorry," Markstein said. "Of course we don't want them to know that we know they're there."

"This is something I'm going to deal with," Clint told him. "You don't need to worry about it."

"Very well."

"Let's get mounted up," Chance said.

"This one's yours, mister," Axel said, handing Markstein the reins of the dun.

"Thank you, Axel."

They mounted up and Axel said, "I wish ya'll luck."

"You'll get your horses back in one piece, Axel," Clint promised.

"I don't have no doubt about that, Mr. Adams," Axel said. "Anybody who's got a horse like yours knows how to take care of 'em."

Clint waved and the three of them rode out of town. Chance took the lead, Markstein was in the middle, and Clint rode drag, leading the packhorse behind him.

"Why should we ride to Beale Springs?" Jeff Kemp asked. His partner, Paul Drake, was standing behind him, nodding.

"Because the word I got is that the mine they're goin' to is the Blue Lady, which is above Beale Springs."

"So why don't we just follow them?" Drake asked.

"Because they'll spot four of us tailin' them," Breckens said. "I want you two to ride ahead with me, and Aaron here will trail them."

"Why me?" Edwards asked.

"Because I'm tellin' you to," Breckens said, "and remember who makes the decisions around here."

"Well, they've already left," Kemp pointed out. "How do we get there ahead of them?"

"They're leadin' a packhorse," Breckens said. "That'll slow them down. And we're gonna circle them and get ahead of them."

"And what if—"

"But we ain't gonna get there first if we stay here askin' questions," Breckens said. "Are we?"

"I guess not," Kemp said.

"So let's just get goin'," Breckens said. "With any luck this job will be done by tomorrow."

"And we'll have our money," Drake said.

"That's right," Breckens said, "we'll all have our money."

# TWENTY-FIVE

"Where will we be stopping to camp?" Clint asked Chance.

"Actually, we'll camp at Beale Springs, and then start up to the mine from there tomorrow morning."

"What is Beale Springs like?" Markstein asked. "Is it a town?"

"Used to be a settlement," Chance said, "then a fort for a few years. There's still water there, but that's pretty much all it is now, a water stop."

"Is Kingman the closest place to get supplies?"

"Mineral Park used to be the place to go for supplies, but since the Atlantic and Pacific railroad came into Kingman, it's become the hub of this area. There's even a rumor that the newspaper—the *Miner*—might move from Mineral Park to Kingman."

They had stopped to rest the horses, so the three men were sitting abreast with the packhorse behind them.

Markstein fidgeted in the saddle and Clint asked, "Are you okay?"

"I'm not used to these western saddles."

"You'll get used to it," Clint told him, but on the other side of Markstein, Chance was rolling his eyes.

"What about the men following us?" Markstein asked. "Are they still there?"

"I only saw one," Chance said. "Strikes me as odd."

"Unless the other one is ahead of us," Clint said.

"Why would they do that?" Markstein asked.

"Split up and take us from two sides," Chance said. He looked at Clint. "What about Beale Springs? What if he's waiting for us there?"

Clint stretched in his saddle and gave it some thought.

"It doesn't make sense for them to split up, unless . . ."

"Unless what?" Markstein asked.

"Unless there's more than two of them," Chance said. "One's tailing us, while two or three or more go ahead of us to Beale Springs to wait and set up an ambush."

"And why would they do this?" Markstein asked.

"Well, they're not after me, so it's one of you," Chance said. "The way I see it, they either want your mine, or they want a chance at the Gunsmith."

"They're not going to get possession of his mine by killing him on the trail," Clint said.

"Unless . . ." Chance said.

"Unless what?" Markstein asked again.

"Unless someone else sent them," Clint said. "Someone who will benefit if you get killed on the trail."

"My God," Markstein said. "You mean . . . my partner? My new partner would try to have me killed?"

"You said only one of them would sell out. What's your partner's name?" Clint asked.

Markstein thought, then said, "I don't know the whole name—all I know is J. English."

"J?" Clint asked. "The letter J?"

"That's all I know."

"Joe," Chance said.

"What?"

"Joe English," Chance said. "That's his partner's name."

"You seem familiar with him," Clint said. "Would this Joe English have Markstein killed in order to take total possession of the mine?"

"I don't think so."

"Why not?"

"Not the type," Chance said.

"Then what kind of type are we dealing with?" Clint asked.

Chance shrugged. "You'll find out when you get there. Let's keep moving."

As they started forward again, Clint asked, "Can we get there and bypass Beale Springs?"

"I'm already thinking about that," Chance said.

# TWENTY-SIX

By the next time they stopped, Chance had a plan. They dismounted to rest the horses—and Markstein. The topography was rocky and hard, with enough boulders for them each to find one to sit on. They passed around a canteen of water while Chance explained.

"Right now we're between the Hualapai and Cerbat mountains," he said. "The Blue Lady is in the Cerbats. I think I know a way to bypass Beale Springs and approach the Cerbat peaks from another direction—if it's clear."

"If it's clear?" Clint asked.

"There's a possibility that the pass I have in mind could have been blocked by an avalanche. We had some bad weather last month, which could have caused it. If it's clear, we'll have a good route to the Cerbats. But if it's blocked, we'll have to double back."

"And if we bypass Beale Springs, we'll have to conserve water, because we won't be able to fill up, right?" Clint asked.

"There might be a cistern of some kind, but technically you're right."

"I would like to get there as soon as possible," Markstein

said. "You could be wrong about the ambush, could you not?"

"Sure we could," Clint said.

"If we're right, there'll be trouble," Chance said.

"Which I'm sure you and Mr. Adams can handle," Markstein said. "After all, I saw what Mr. Adams did to that fellow Dolan."

"That was one man," Chance said. "We don't know how many we might be facing at Beale Springs."

"It could be only one more, right?" Markstein asked.

"Or two, or three, or a dozen," Clint said.

"Well," Markstein said, "there must be a way to find out."

"Sure," Chance said, "name it."

Markstein stared at the two of them for a few moments, then asked, "Why don't we ask him?"

"Ask who?" Chance said.

"The one who's behind us."

Clint looked past Markstein at Buck Chance and said, "Why don't we ask him?"

"I suppose we could," Chance said. "If we change direction, we won't want him tailing us, anyway."

"One of us could circle around behind him," Clint said, "get the drop on him."

"There's a place just ahead, a dip, where he'll lose sight of us for a few moments," Chance said. "One of us could break off then and circle around."

"Once he sees that there's only two of us, he'll get suspicious, figure something's up," Clint said.

"Then whichever one of us it is will have to move fast," Chance said. "That means me."

"You can move faster than me?" Clint asked.

Chance looked at him.

"You're faster with a gun, and you have the faster horse," Chance said, "but I'm younger and faster on my feet than you are."

Markstein looked at Clint and said, "I believe he might be right."

Clint took only a few seconds, then said, "Yeah, well, okay, he might be right."

"I won't even have to circle around," Chance said. "I can climb up on top of a boulder and then knock him off his horse."

"What if we capture the fellow and he won't talk?" Markstein asked.

Clint and Chance exchanged a look, and then Clint said, "Oh, he'll talk."


Aaron Edwards was angry that this thankless job had fallen to him. If the three men were heading for Beale Springs, why couldn't they all have just gone on ahead? What was the good of trailing them?

All they did was ride and rest, ride and rest.

He lost sight of them now up ahead for a few moments, and then they came back into view. Once he entered that dip, he'd lose them again for a few seconds, but they were always there, just ahead of him . . . Wait, was that a riderless horse?

Before he could figure out what that meant, he was hit from the side and snatched right off his horse.

# TWENTY-SEVEN

As soon as Chance hit the man and pulled him from his horse, Clint handed the reins of the packhorse to Markstein and rode back to help. By the time he reached the two men, though, Chance had the other unarmed, the gun stuck into his belt, and had a knee in his back. He also had a gash in his chin where he'd struck the rocks.

"Need help?" Clint asked.

"It would be nice," Chance said. "I'd like to stop the blood that's gushing from my chin."

Clint dismounted, approached the two men and examined Chance's wound.

"Don't be a baby," he said. "It's not gushing."

"Hey, what about me?" the man on the bottom demanded. "My back hurts."

"You I don't care about," Clint said. "Just shut up and don't talk until we're ready to talk to you."

"I don't know what's goin' on—"

Chance slapped the man on the back of the head, causing his forehead to bounce off the hard ground.

"The man told you to shut up!"

"My friend is going to take his knee out of your back," Clint said. "I want you to stay where you are."

"Why can't I get—"

"If you move at all, I'll shoot you."

That shut the man up, but only for a moment.

"You wouldn't—"

"Try me," Clint said. "My friend and I don't like being followed. If I don't shoot you, he will."

"You got all that?" Chance asked.

The man didn't respond.

"You want me to hit you on the back of the head again?" Chance demanded.

"I thought you didn't want me to talk," the man whined.

"Talk when you're talked to," Chance said. "Got it?"

"Okay, okay, I got it."

Chance removed his knee from the man's back and stood up. The man immediately tried to run. He scrambled up, but before he could get very far Clint drew and fired. His bullet took the heel of the man's right boot clean off.

"Jesus!" The man fell to the ground and grabbed for his foot, convinced it had been shot off. "You shot me!"

"I told you I was going to shoot you if you tried to run," Clint said. "Maybe you understand that now?"

"Yeah, yeah," the man said, "I understand." He looked at his foot and heaved a sigh of relief to see that it was still there. Then he realized what Clint had done. "You shot my heel off."

"I was aiming for your ankle," Clint told him. He ejected the spent shell, reloaded and holstered the weapon.

Chance had a bandana pressed to his chin.

"Who's gonna question him?" he asked Clint.

"I will," Clint said. "You're bleeding too much."

"You told me I wasn't bleeding that bad!"

"I lied. I guess you might be younger and quicker, but you bruise easily. You better take care of it."

Clint looked at the man seated on the ground.

"What's your name?"

The man did not reply.

"You want the other heel shot off?" Clint asked. He touched his gun. "Maybe this time I'll actually hit your ankle."

"No," the man said, putting his hands out to ward off a bullet. "My name's Edwards, Aaron Edwards."

"And what are you doing following us?"

Clint could see Edwards trying to decide what to say. He decided to help him by drawing his gun and cocking the hammer back.

"Okay, okay," Edwards said. "It wasn't my idea, it was Carl's."

"Carl who?"

"Breckens."

Clint looked at Chance who, still holding the bandana to his wound, shook his head. From behind them they could hear Markstein, who had finally maneuvered his mount and the packhorse over to them.

"We don't know him," Clint said. "Who is he?"

"He's . . . just a guy I ride with."

"And why is he having you follow us?"

"Because he went ahead to Beale Springs to wait."

"Wait for us?"

Edwards nodded.

"Is he alone?"

"No, he has two other men with him," Edwards said. "If you want their names, you'll have to gimme a minute to think."

"That's not necessary," Clint said. "Who or what are they after?"

Edwards used his chin to point and said, "Him."

Clint and Chance turned and looked at Markstein, who was still mounted.

"Me? Why me?"

"He wants your mine."

"And he's willing to kill to get it?" Clint asked.

"Yeah—well, not him, so much. The guy who hired us is."

"You were hired to kill me?" Markstein asked.

"Yes."

"By who?" Clint asked. "Exactly who?"

"I dunno."

"Edwards—"

"I really don't," the man said. "Carl does all the thinkin' for us."

"And all the negotiating," Chance said.

"Right."

"So you have no idea who hired you?"

"No," Edwards said. "I was just goin' along with Carl, who said we'd get paid a lot of money."

"Why the other two men?" Clint asked.

"Once Carl realized we were gonna have to deal with you and him," Edwards said, indicating Chance, "he figured we needed some help."

Clint turned to look at Chance and Markstein.

"Any questions?" he asked them.

"Not for him," Markstein said, "but I have a few for you."

"Not in front of him," Clint said. "They'll have to wait until we get on the trail again. Chance, how long would it take this fella to walk to Beale Springs."

"With only one heel on his boot? He'd be lucky to get there tomorrow mornin'."

"What?" Edwards said. "Walk? I can't walk—"

"Would you rather be tied up out here?" Clint asked.

"Well, no—"

"Or dead?" Chance asked.

"Hell, no!"

"Then you'll walk," Clint said. He looked at Chance. "You up to watching this jasper while I retrieve his horse and yours?"

"Sure, why not?" He looked at his bandana. "I think the bleeding stopped. Ain't so bad."

"Good."

Clint mounted up and caught both horses. Once Chance was mounted, he gave him the reins of Edwards's horse while he grabbed the pack animal again.

"Ya can't leave me here," Edwards said. "I'll die."

"You won't die," Chance said. "If you walk back the way we came, you'll get to Kingman faster than you'd get to Beale Springs."

"Gimme a gun, man," he said. "There's mountain lions out here."

"No gun," Clint said.

"B-but . . . at least leave me some water."

Clint reached over and took the canteen from Edwards's saddle. It felt half full. He tossed it to the man.

"Drink sparingly," he advised. To Markstein and Chance he said, "Let's go."

# TWENTY-EIGHT

When they had ridden along the trail a ways, Clint stopped so Markstein could ask his questions.

"Go ahead, George," Clint said.

"How do we get to the mine without getting killed?" the man asked. "And then once we get there—if we get there—how do we find out who hired someone to kill me?"

"Is that all?" Clint asked.

"For now."

"I think Chance can help us with the first part," Clint said. "We're going to need that alternate route."

"Don't forget I told you it might be blocked," Chance said.

"We'll deal with that if and when the time comes," Clint said.

"Why not just go to Beale Springs and have it out with those men?" Markstein asked. "After all, you—" He stopped short.

"I . . . what, George?" Clint asked.

"Well, you are who you are."

"That's exactly why there are extra men waitin' there," Chance said. "And we only have that jasper's word that there are only three. We could be walkin' into a dozen guns."

"I see."

"Don't worry," Clint said. "Once we get to the mine, we'll find out who's putting up money to have you killed. After all, they've pretty much paid to have me and Chance killed, too. I don't know about him, but that doesn't sit well with me."

"Me, neither."

Clint looked at Chance and saw a trickle of blood come down from beneath his hat.

"Let's take care of that gash on your head," he said. "We don't want to leave a blood trail behind us."

"May I step down as well?" Markstein asked as Clint and Chance dismounted.

"Yes," Clint said, "step down and rest while I perform some first aid on our friend."

Markstein dismounted and walked around a bit, rubbing his butt with both hands.

Chance took a seat on a boulder and Clint tore a shirt he'd found in Edwards's saddlebags into strips.

"Is that clean?" Chance asked. "He didn't look too clean."

"It's a clean shirt," Clint assured him, although he didn't know for sure. He wasn't about to smell it to find out.

He wrapped some of the shirt around Chance's head and then tied it off in a makeshift bandage.

"Your hat will help keep it on," Clint said.

"Thanks. Can I ask you somethin'?"

"Sure."

"Why didn't we just kill that fella instead of leavin' him around?"

"I don't do things that way. Besides, he's not going to get anywhere fast where he can hurt us."

"Maybe not."

Clint stood up.

"We're going to have to get rid of his horse."

"I can unsaddle it now and let it loose," Chance said, also standing.

"No, not yet," Clint said. "Let's get farther along. It might find its way back to him."

"Good point."

"How long before we head off to your alternate route?"

"I'm not sure," Chance said. "We may have to wait 'til mornin' if we don't find it soon. I don't know if we can navigate it in the dark. We don't want a horse breakin' its leg."

"Then perhaps we should keep his horse as a spare," Markstein said.

"Nope," Chance said. "We're not gonna be able to take it with us. In fact, we might have to cut the packhorse loose, too. We're not gonna be on anything even closely resembling a trail."

"It sounds like we might get killed just taking this short-cut," Markstein said.

"Only if you fall off the side of the mountain," Chance said.

# TWENTY-NINE

Markstein didn't fall off the side of the mountain, but he did almost topple over once, and it was because he was fighting his horse. His riding in the East had not prepared him for riding up the side of a mountain.

Chance had found his shortcut before the light faded. As they started up, Markstein began to have problems, which Clint could see because they were riding single file with Chance ahead of Markstein, and Clint once again taking up the rear with the pack animal.

"Hold up!" he shouted to Chance, who was getting farther ahead of them.

"There's a clearing I know of that I want to reach before dark," Chance shouted back.

"Okay," Clint said. "Keep going. We'll catch up."

Chance nodded, and continued on.

Clint rode up alongside Markstein, who had reined his horse in.

"You're fighting your animal, George."

"I'm trying to show him where the best footing is," Markstein said. "I don't want to fall."

"He is finding the best footing, and you're yanking him

back," Clint said. "If you fall, it'll be your fault, not his. Just give him his head and let him find his own way."

"Okay."

"Don't fight him," Clint said. "Fight the urge and put your faith in him."

"I'll try."

The rest of the way went better because Markstein was able to stop fighting his mare. Eventually they reached the clearing Chance had spoken about, and he already had a fire going.

"Wasn't that easier?" Clint asked Markstein as they dismounted.

"Not easy," the other man said, "but easier, yes."

"Just put your trust in your horse," Clint said.

"I'll remember."

"I'll bed them down," Clint said. "You sit at the fire and have a cup of coffee."

"Thank you."

Markstein sat by the fire and accepted a cup from Chance. He sipped it and shuddered, it was that strong. The second sip, however, did not engender the same reaction.

"Won't the fire give us away?"

"They can't see our fire from Beale Springs," Chance said. "My guess is they'll be waitin' there until mornin', and then they'll probably go looking for Edwards."

"And when they find him?"

"It'll be too late for them to do anything. We'll be at the mining camp. If they still want to kill you, they'll have to do it there."

"Somehow I don't find that very comforting."

"It wasn't meant to be," Chance said. "I'm gonna make some bacon and beans."

Markstein made a face but resigned himself to the fact that he was in the West now. And he would only be there long enough to make himself wealthy—or wealthier—before returning home as the purveyor of the finest turquoise stones in the country.

If he lived long enough.


"I smell bacon and beans," Clint said, arriving at the fire. "And if I'm not mistaken, that smells like good trail coffee."

"I like it strong," Chance said. "Sorry."

"I think it melted my teeth," Markstein complained, but held his cup out for more.

"That's just the way I like it," Clint said, gratefully accepting a cup and a plate.

As they were eating, Chance said, "I can take the first watch."

"Why do we need a watch if they can't find us up here?" Markstein asked.

"Just to be safe," Clint said. "We don't want anybody sneaking up on us while we're asleep. It's embarrassing."

"And deadly," Chance said.

Markstein looked at the sky.

"I must tell you both I never expected to be out here under the stars eating bacon and beans and drinking this strong and curiously good coffee."

"What did you expect?" Chance said.

"Foolishly," he said, "I expected a big hotel room, and I envisioned meeting with my partner in a fine restaurant. I did not expect that my new partner would try to have me killed."

"We still don't know that it's your new partner who put up the money to have you—us—killed," Clint pointed out. "When we get to the camp, we're going to find out, though."

Clint looked across the fire at Chance.

"Once we get there, your job is done, Chance," Clint said. "I guess you can head back."

"Nah," Chance said, "if you fellas don't mind, I think I'll stick around awhile, see how this plays out. Besides, I'd hate to leave you both up there and then hear that you got yourselves killed."

"That's very . . . decent of you," Markstein said.

"Any more coffee there?" Clint asked.

"Yes, I'll have some more, too, please."

"There's plenty," Chance said, "and I can make more."

# THIRTY

The headquarters of the Blue Lady Mine was a cabin that could have been divided into three rooms, but was actually just one large one. When it was built, it was the joint decision of the partners to have it be just one large work space.

Ed Martin sat behind the desk that was in the center of the room. He had blueprints spread out over the entire surface and was tracing the path the new tunnels would take when the door opened and Joe English entered.

"The new partner get here yet?" Martin asked.

"Not yet," English said. "Maybe he fell off the mountain on the way up here from Kingman."

Martin looked up from the blueprints. He'd been hired by both partners to be the foreman of the mine. Or the manager, whichever term suited him. Now that one partner had sold out, he wondered if the new one was going to try to make any changes.

"Maybe that wouldn't be so bad," he said.

"I didn't really mean it," English said. "I'm just frustrated."

"You want to take a look at these new tunnels?"

"Why bother?" English asked. "The contract says that

both partners have to agree to any changes or additions. We might as well wait for him to get here."

"It'll give us somethin' to do," Martin said.

English sighed, then said, "Yeah, okay, why not?" and walked to the desk.

As they broke camp, Markstein was trying to stretch out the kinks from sleeping on the ground. On top of that his butt still hurt from riding with a western saddle.

"You okay?" Chance asked as he kicked dirt onto the fire.

"I don't think I'll ever be able to stand up straight again," Markstein said.

"Well, I'd say that you'll get used to it, but I don't think you'll have to. I don't see you doin' this a lot."

"Good God, no," Markstein said. "I hope there's someplace for me to sleep at the mine other than the ground."

Clint came walking over, leading all the horses, having saddled them himself.

"Are we ready to go?" he asked.

"I am as ready as I'll ever be," Markstein said, accepting the reins of his horse. "At least no one tried to murder us in our sleep."

"Now if nobody tries to murder you in camp, you'll be doin' okay," Chance said.

Clint and Buck exchanged a glance, as they both knew there was small chance of that.

When they reached the all-important pass Chance had been talking about, it was, thankfully, open but it was not rideable.

"We'll have to walk the horses through," Chance said. "When we get to the other side, we'll be on the Cerbats, where your mine is."

"We can only lead one horse at a time," Clint said. "Do we want to tie the packhorse to the last horse?"

"It's liable to step in a hole and snap a leg," Chance said. "Better off just cuttin' it loose."

"What about the supplies?" Markstein asked.

"We can each take some, and leave the rest behind. We'll be at the mine tonight."

They salvaged what they could carry and left the rest on the ground. Then Clint removed the bridle from the packhorse and slapped the animal on the rump. It trotted away a few yards, then turned and looked back at them balefully.

"Looks like he might follow us," Markstein said.

"That'll be up to him," Chance said. "He might go back the way we came. Either way, he's better off."

"He might still snap a leg," Markstein said.

"Yeah," Chance said, "but we won't know."

They each took the reins of their own horse in hand and started through the pass.

"What the fuck?" Carl Breckens said. Ahead of him, walking with a limp, was Aaron Edwards.

Edwards heard the horses behind him and turned to see who it was.

"Jesus," he said to Breckens, "thank God it's you, Carl."

Breckens reined in, the other two men doing the same behind him. They were tired of listening to Breckens bellyache about how useless Edwards was. They each harbored the hope that when they found the man Breckens would just shoot him.

"What the hell happened?" Breckens demanded. "Why are you limpin'? And where's your horse and your gun?"

"They took 'em," Edwards said. "They only left me with my canteen."

"And where's that?"

"I threw it away," Edwards said. "I—it was empty."

"Where did Adams go? And the dandy?"

"I don't know," Edwards said. "They caught me following them, and Adams shot the heel off my boot."

"They caught you? And what did you tell 'em?"

"I didn't tell 'em nothin', Carl."

"Nothin'?" Breckens asked. "Then why'd they let you go? That's Clint Adams we're talkin' about. He'd as soon shoot ya as look at ya."

"Clint Adams?" Kemp said.

"We didn't know nothin' about no Clint Adams," Drake complained.

"I didn't wanna scare ya," Breckens said. "I was gonna tell you before we killed him."

"We gotta get paid more if we're gonna face the Gunsmith," Kemp said.

"Yeah," his partner said.

"Paid more?" Breckens demanded. He looked down at Edwards, who was sweating and nervous and couldn't stand straight because of his missing boot heel.

"You didn't tell them a thing?"

"I swear."

"I don't believe you."

Breckens drew his gun and fired once. The bullet hit Edwards in the chest and shattered his heart. He went sprawling onto the ground, arms stretched out, no longer sweating or worried.

Breckens holstered his gun and turned to look at the other two men, who were staring down at the body.

"You want more money?" he asked them.

"Uh, yeah," Drake said.

"You can have his share."

Kemp and Drake looked at each other.

"Just don't disappoint me the way he did," Breckens added.

# THIRTY-ONE

Once they made it through the pass without incident, they were able to mount up again and make good time to the Blue Lady Mine region of the Cerbat Mountain range. They passed the sites of several other mines. And when they passed a large tent, Clint asked Chance about it.

"Two fellas stocked up on supplies, came up here, erected the tent and now they run a combination saloon and general store. This way, instead of each mine sending someone down to Kingman for supplies, these two fellas do it, and the mining operations get their supplies from them."

"Sounds like what Bullock and his partner did in Deadwood," Clint said.

"Deadwood eventually became a town," Chance said. "I don't think that'll be the case up here."

"Why not?" Markstein asked.

"Look around," Chance said. "The terrain just wouldn't support it. There's no room to spread out."

"Not even if all the mining operations operated under one owner?" Markstein asked.

"Is that your plan?" Chance asked. "To buy up all the mines and run them together?"

"My plan was to buy a piece of a mine up here," Markstein said. "That was it. The Blue Lady became available— half of it, anyway—and I jumped at the opportunity. That's the extent of my plans at the moment."

"Why?" Clint asked Chance. "Do you know of anyone else up here who wants to sell out?"

"Just the opposite," Chance said. "These folks have a good thing going and they don't wanna get rid of it. I think they're all surprised that someone sold out, even a piece of a mine."

Up ahead they spotted a cabin with a sign above the door that read BLUE LADY MINE.

"There's your place," Chance said.

There were other, smaller structures orbiting the larger one, presumably bunkhouses or homes for the mine owners.

They rode up to the larger building and dismounted. Markstein was sore head to toe from riding and from sleeping on the ground. He groaned as he dismounted. Clint and Chance shared a laugh.

"You think this is funny?" Markstein asked. "I may never walk right again, and you think this is funny?"

"We were just thinkin' that you've loosened up some since we took you on the trail," Chance said.

"That's right," Clint said, catching on. "You're not the stiff easterner you were when you arrived in Kingman."

"I'm not?" he asked. "Seems to me I'm stiffer than I've ever been." He stared at them, then smiled.

"See?" Chance said. "You got it. You've developed a sense of humor, George."

"Is that what being close to death does to you?" he asked.

"Every time," Clint said. "It's the only way to get through it."

They tied their horses off at the hitching post in front of the building and walked to the front door.

"Just knock and go in," Chance said. "That's what they expect."

Markstein knocked and opened the door and the three men trooped in. There were two men standing behind a desk, looking down, and both their heads snapped up at the sound of boots.

"Help you gents?" the older one asked. He had salt-and-pepper hair and mustache, and was built thick through the chest.

"My name is George Markstein, and I believe you work for me."

"Mr. Markstein," the man said, coming around from behind the desk with his hand extended. "It's a pleasure to meet you, sir. My name is Ed Martin. I believe we corresponded."

"Yes, we did," Markstein said, "but only because my partner refused to do so."

The two men shook briefly.

"Yeah, well, Joe English can be a little stubborn. You'll be wanting to meet, though."

"As soon as possible," Markstein said.

"No time like the present," Martin said. He turned to the younger man. "Go get Joe, will ya, Dan? And don't say why."

"Sure, boss."

The young man named Dan made his way through the three strangers and out the door.

"This is Clint Adams," Markstein said. "He saved my life when I got into some trouble in Kingman."

"Really?" Martin looked at Clint. "The Gunsmith?"

"That's right."

"Well," he said to Markstein, "I guess it's lucky for you he was around."

"Indeed. And I believe you know this gentleman."

"Sure. Hi, Chance. I figure you for the guide, right?"

"That's right."

"Well," Martin said, "when Joe gets here, we can have a drink to, uh, celebrate."

Markstein walked to the desk.

"Are these blueprints of the mine?"

"Uh, those are blueprints for proposed new shafts," Martin said, walking around behind the desk.

Markstein walked around to join him, pressed his palms to the desktop and leaned down to have a look. Ed Martin backed off in deference to his new boss.

Clint, for want of something better to do, looked around the large one-room office. There was a second, smaller desk against the wall on one side that looked as if it didn't get used much. In another corner some equipment was stacked. In another corner, a file cabinet.

The door opened behind him and he heard someone enter.

"Ah. Here's Joe," Ed Martin said. "Joe, this here's your new partner, George Markstein. Mr. Markstein, this is Joe English."

George Markstein looked shocked. Clint turned, took one look at Joe English and felt his own jaw drop. He looked over at Chance, who was smirking with delight.

"That is my partner?" Markstein asked.

"You're Joe English?" Clint asked.

"Yep," Chance said, "that's who it is."

"Oh, well," Martin said, "I guess you gents didn't know—"

"Never mind explaining, Ed," Joe English said, slamming the door. "They know now, and if they don't like it that's their problem."

Clint stepped forward, put out his hand and said, "Clint Adams. I'm happy to meet you."

"I know that name," English said. "The Gunsmith, right?"

"That's right."

"Well, what an unexpected pleasure." Clint felt his hand being taken in a firm grasp. "My name is Joanne English," the beautiful blond woman said.

# THIRTY-TWO

"Hello, Buck."

"Joe."

"Your friends look like they've never seen a woman before," she said.

"I'm willin' to bet they ain't never seen a woman like you before, Joe," Chance said.

"You're always the flatterer, Buck."

She released Clint's hand after giving it an extra squeeze, then walked past him.

"I suppose you're my new partner," she said to Markstein. "I guess you know I wasn't happy about Hector selling out to you."

"I gathered that, Miss . . . is it Miss?"

"It is."

"Miss English," Markstein said. "Your refusal to correspond with me made that very clear."

"Yeah, well," she said, "I suppose the best thing to do now is try to get along."

"I hope that's how you really feel, Miss English," Markstein said.

"What's that supposed to mean?" she demanded. "I usually say what I mean."

"He means that somebody hired some guns to kill him before he could get here," Clint said.

Joe English turned on Clint.

"And you think it was me?"

"We don't know who it is," Clint said. "All we know is that you didn't want him as a partner."

She glared at Clint. He could see the fine lines around her eyes and her mouth. She was closer to forty than thirty, but was still one of the most attractive women he'd ever seen—especially now that she was angry.

"You've got a lot of nerve," she snapped. "I'll have you know I didn't want anyone as a partner, not Mr. Markstein, specifically. I have nothing against him, and would not try to kill him. I'd be more likely to try and buy him out."

"Not much chance of that, I'm afraid," Markstein said, "but my last offer to buy you out still stands, Miss English."

"Not a chance," she said, whirling on him and away from Clint, "so I guess we're just stuck with each other for a while."

"Fine," Markstein said. "I'd like to talk about these blueprints."

"Now?" she asked. "You just got here. I can have someone show you to your quarters so you can get some rest."

"Yes, well," he said, "I am rather tired. Mr. Adams will also need some quarters—"

"We've got nothing," she said. She turned to look at Clint. "Sorry, but we never figured on entertaining guests up here. You can do what Chance does when he comes up here."

Clint looked at Chance.

"Bedroll," he said with a shrug.

"You're welcome to eat with us," she said. "We'll be doing that in about an hour. In the morning breakfast is at six."

"Thanks for the hospitality," Clint said.

She studied him for a moment to see if he was being sarcastic, then decided he wasn't.

"You're welcome." She turned to look at Martin. "Ed, have someone show Mr. Markstein where he sleeps."

"Sure, boss."

"Chance? You know where to bed down?" she asked.

"Yep."

"You staying with us?"

"For a while."

She looked at Clint.

"The men who were going to try to kill Markstein were going to try to kill me, too," Clint explained. "Also Chance. I think we'll stick around to make sure Markstein doesn't catch a bullet in the back. If that's okay."

"I insist on it," she said. "Over supper you can tell me who these men are and how they tried to kill you."

"Be my pleasure," Clint said.

"Come on, Clint," Chance said. "We can take care of the horses and I'll show you where we bed down."

"George?" Clint said.

"I think I should be all right here in camp for a while, Clint."

"We'll keep him alive," Joe English said, "if just to prove that it's not me trying to kill him."

"Fair enough," Clint said.

Clint followed Chance outside, where they untied all three horses and led them away.

"You're a sonofabitch, you know that?" Clint asked him.

"I don't know what you're talkin' about."

"You knew that Joe English was a woman," Clint accused, "and a damned beautiful one."

"Hey, I didn't know you didn't know."

"Yeah, sure."

"She is beautiful, though, isn't she?"

"Anything going on there, Chance?"

Chance looked surprised.

"What? With me and Joe? I wish. She don't look at me twice. I think she thinks I'm too young for her."

"What are you, thirty?"

"Almost."

"And she must be almost forty."

Chance's eyes bugged. "You think so?"

Apparently he hadn't thought she was that old.

"Yeah, I think so."

They walked a few paces and then Clint said, "Tell me about this Ed Martin."

"Solid mining man," Chance said. "He's managed a couple of operations, but he's been with Joe from the beginning."

"The beginning?"

"Three years ago, she and her partner, Hector Ramirez, hit it big. Martin's been manager from the start."

"How'd she get along with her partner?"

"He was an old friend of her father's," Chance said. "When he sold out, she felt betrayed. Can't say I blame her."

"What about her and Martin."

"What about them? Oh, you mean—naw, I don't think there's anythin' between them. Joe's got no time for anythin' like that."

They came to a clearing just out of sight of the cabin. Clint could see where old campfires had burned.

"This'll do," he said.

"Why all the questions about Joe?" Chance asked as they unsaddled their mounts. "You interested?"

"I just met the woman, Chance."

Chance laughed and said, "Oh yeah, you're interested."

# THIRTY-THREE

"What kind of quarters do you have?" Clint asked George Markstein over supper.

"A cabin," Markstein said. "A little rustic, but it will do."

Clint, Markstein and Chance were sitting at a table in a cabin that had been set up as a mess hall for the miners. Sitting with them were Joe English and Ed Martin.

Their table was the center of attention—and conversation—as the miners checked out their new boss. Word had also gotten around about who Clint was, and he was drawing a lot of curious stares.

"So tell me, Mr. Adams," Joe English said, "what attempts have been made on Mr. Markstein?"

"Well," Clint said, "the first . . ."

He told her about Mike Dolan, which might or might not have been a setup to make it look like Markstein had been killed in a stupid argument over a room. Then he told her about the men who had been following them, and how they had tried to set up an ambush at Beale Springs.

When he was done, she turned to Markstein.

"Look, Mr. Markstein—"

"George," he said, "please."

"George," she said, "I don't know any of these men. I would never ask somebody to try to kill you."

"That's very—" Markstein started, but she cut him off.

"If I wanted you dead," she went on, "I'd kill you myself."

That seemed to shock Markstein and he sat up straight for a moment and stared at her. She was sitting across from him, and he was sitting to Clint's right. Chance was on Clint's left. Ed Martin was sitting to Joe's right.

"You know," Markstein said, finally, "I think you mean that."

"Oh, I do."

"Well," Clint said, "that certainly clears the air."

"And leaves the question," Chance said, "who did hire those men to kill George?"

"That's a question we're going to find the answer to," Clint said, "before we leave this camp."

"Why would anyone be foolish enough to try to kill George," Joe asked, "if they knew they'd have to face you at the same time?"

"Two reasons," Clint said. "One is money."

"And the second?"

"Most men are reputation hunters," Clint said. "That makes me a big target."

"What a way to live," Joe said, shaking her head.

"It's the only way I have."

They ate in silence for a few moments, and then Markstein said, "The men seem . . . curious."

"Yes," she said. "About Clint Adams, and about you. They wonder if you're going to want to make any changes, if their jobs are safe."

"Surely I can't make any wholesale changes without your agreement."

She stared at him.

"Maybe you didn't read your contract as carefully as you think, Mr. Markstein," she said.

"Oh?"

"My partner sold you fifty-one percent of this mine," she said. "I own the other forty-nine."

"I am senior partner," Markstein said.

"Yes."

Clint studied Joe English. He was having second thoughts about whether or not she had hired Breckens to kill Markstein. Surely him being senior partner was motive enough.

"Well," Markstein said, "that doesn't sound right to me, Miss English."

"What do you suggest, then?"

"I suggest you buy one percent from me," Markstein replied. "That way we will be equal partners."

She looked surprised.

"You would do that?"

"I think it's only fair."

"It's more than fair," she said. "Thank you, George."

"You're welcome . . . Joe."

After supper Joe English stood up and introduced George Markstein as her partner. Markstein then addressed the miners and told them that all their jobs were safe.

"In fact," he added, "with the new shafts being considered, there will probably be new jobs available."

"When will we know that, sir?" someone asked.

"I have to go over the blueprints with Miss English and Mr. Martin," Markstein said. "As soon as I'm fully informed, we'll let you all know what's happening. Meanwhile it's business as usual. Thank you."

There was a smattering of applause, but clearly everyone's minds were not put at ease.

Outside the mess hall Markstein said to Joe, "I don't think I put their minds at ease at all."

"Well, they'll just have to wait and see what happens," she said. "Like the rest of us."

"Would you like to look at those blueprints now?" Ed Martin asked Markstein.

"Yes," he said, then looked at Joe and added, "You draw up some papers for the sale of that one percent. I meant what I said."

"All right," she said, "I will."

As Markstein walked away with Ed Martin, Joe English asked Clint, "Is he for real?"

"Like you said," he replied, "I guess we'll just have to wait and see."

"Can I buy you a drink?" she asked.

# THIRTY-FOUR

Joe led Clint to the tent Chance had told him was half saloon, half general store. When they got inside, he saw what
Chance had meant. One side of the tent was a counter and
merchandise, while the other side was a small bar and a
few tables, most of which were now taken since supper was
over, and so was the day's work.

Miners made a place for their boss and her guest, and
she got two beers from the bartender.

"I can't believe he'd give up controlling interest in the
mine," she said to Clint.

"I can't explain it."

"It's not good business."

"Well, from what I know of him—which isn't much—he
appears to be a successful businessman."

"Well then, he's got a funny way of running his business,"
she said.

"Why don't you just draw up the papers as quickly as
you can, just in case," he suggested.

"I think that's probably a good idea."

A man came walking over, smiling broadly at Joe, ignor-
ing Clint.

"Joe, it's so nice to see you in here," he said, taking her free hand. "You don't come in a lot."

"I was just showing the place to our guest, Isaac," she said. The way she slipped her hand from his gave Clint the feeling she hadn't enjoyed the physical contact with the man.

"Clint, this is Isaac Brown, one of the owners of this little establishment. Isaac, this is Clint Adams."

Brown looked at Clint, actually seeing him for the first time. The merchant appeared to be in his forties, tall, well-fed, but not fat.

"Clint Adams . . . the Gunsmith?" the man asked.

"That's right."

"Well, what brings such a famous gunman to our little corner of the mountain?" Brown asked.

Clint allowed the word "gunman" to go by without comment.

"Mr. Adams is a friend of my new partner, and brought him here safely from Kingman."

"Safely?" Brown asked. "Was there any reason to think that he wouldn't get here safely?"

"There was some indication of that, yes," Clint said.

"They encountered some trouble on the trail, but managed to avoid anything violent."

"I see," Brown said. "Do you think the trouble may follow you up here?"

"It's possible," Clint said.

"Well, maybe we ought to send for the sheriff."

"Let's not overreact," Joe said. "I think if there's any trouble, Clint will be able to handle it."

"Yes, you're probably right about that. Well, then we're glad to have you around, Mr. Adams." The man turned his gaze toward Joe. "You should come around here more often, young lady. You dress up the place."

She smiled but didn't say anything, and he walked away.

"You don't like him very much, do you?" Clint asked.

"No," she said, "he's . . . slimy, like a snake-oil sales-man." Then she put her hand to her mouth. "Was it that obvious?"

"No, it wasn't," Clint said. "I just have a feel for that kind of thing. The way you slid your hand out of his, the way you stood . . ."

"You're very observant," she said.

"It helps in staying alive."

"What are your days like?" she asked. "Having to worry about that day in, day out?"

"You get used to it after a while."

"Really?"

"No, not really," he said, "but you learn to live with it."

"Why not take your gun off and be done with it?"

He smiled.

"I'd be dead in minutes if I did that."

"I suppose that was naïve of me," she said. "It's a way of life you're stuck with. I know something about that."

"Oh? Are you stuck up here?"

"It's the only way of life I've ever known," she said. "My father was a miner, and he made sure I was one. Luckily, I don't have to actually work underground."

"Why don't you sell and go on to something else, then?" he asked. Then hurriedly added, "Not that I'm urging you to sell—"

"I understand the question, Clint," she said. "I can't sell. This was my father's dream, a successful mine. Of course, he was thinking about gold, not turquoise, but this is what I found."

"But is it a way of life you hate?"

She made a face, almost as if the question pained her—or maybe it was the answer.

"I don't hate it, but I wonder about what else is out there. I'm in my midthirties—I know, I look older—and

I'd like to think I'd get to see a little more of the world, or, at least, of this country before I die."

He decided not to address the question of her looking older. Fact was, she was a beautiful woman, and she had to know that.

She swirled the beer at the bottom of her glass, staring at it, then drank it down.

"I think I'll go to my cabin and turn in," she said.

"Well, good night then—"

"Would you like to come along?"

"To your cabin?"

"Yes, to my cabin."

Clint wanted to make sure he was reading her right.

"And that would be for . . ."

"Sex, what else?" she said. "Look, I don't have time to be coy. I haven't had sex in a very long time, and I can't sleep with any of the men up here. I'm the boss. I need someone who's not going to be here for very long."

"Well, I—"

"It's a yes or no question, Clint Adams," she said. "Don't make me ask again."

"Well then . . . yes."

# THIRTY-FIVE

Joe was wearing a man's shirt and baggy pants, which did nothing to hide the fullness of her body. But Clint's breath still caught when she allowed him to peel the clothing from her. Her breasts were pale, almost pear-shaped, with large nipples and wide areole. He slid his hands beneath her so that her breasts were resting in his palms, and loved the feel of their weight. Holding them like that, he thumbed her nipples until she bit her lips and squirmed.

Her face and hands were dark from the sun, but the rest of her body was pale white—so pale that he could see the light blue veins beneath the surface. He pulled off her boots, and then discarded her pants, made her turn so he could run his hands over her buttocks and kiss them, run his tongue up along the crack between her cheeks. She squirmed some more, worked her way over to the bed and crawled onto it. He had no choice but to follow, but she used her feet and her legs to fend him off.

"Oh no," she said, "you can't come into this bed with your clothes on. Take 'em off."

"Yes, ma'am."

He was still wearing his gun. There was no bedpost to hang the holster from, so he hung it on the back of a wooden chair and pulled the chair closer to the bed. She watched him do this without saying a word.

The gun within easy reach, he then removed the rest of his clothes and got into the bed with her.

Ed Martin traced his forefinger along one of the proposed shafts, explaining his thinking to George Markstein, who listened intently.

". . . then we'd hook up to this one here and cut across this way. By doing that, we come at the deposit from both directions."

"Well," Markstein said as Martin stood straight up, "you certainly know your business."

"I've been in these mountains for a long time, first looking for gold, then finding copper and mining it and, finally, finding the turquoise. I worked for a long time with Joe and with her father, Walter."

"So you must have a good relationship with her," Markstein said.

Ed Martin looked at Markstein quickly, to see if he meant anything by that, and was apparently satisfied that he did not.

"Walter was like a father to me, and Joe's like a sister. Did you mean what you said about selling her that one percent?"

"I did."

"Why?"

"I think it's only fair we be full partners," Markstein said. "Don't you?"

"Of course."

For a moment Markstein wondered if Martin wanted to make an offer on the one percent. If he was like family to Joe and her father, why did he not own even that much of it?

"I like what I see here," Markstein said, turning his attention back to the blueprints, "but I have some questions and some suggestions about—well, here, let me show you . . ."

• • •

Carl Breckens was sitting alone on one side of the fire while Kemp and Drake were seated across from him. Neither man had said very much to him since he'd shot down Aaron Edwards in cold blood.

Breckens was angry, and his anger was directed at everyone but himself. It was everyone else's fault that the dandy from the East wasn't dead yet, not his. When he got to the camp, he was going to make sure the job got done once and for all, even if it meant shooting Clint Adams in the back first to get him out of the way.

"You boys take the watch," he said.

"Watch for what?" Kemp asked. "They're ahead of us, right?"

"Maybe," Breckens said. "Edwards wasn't sure which way they'd gone, and I don't want any surprises during the night. So one of you take first watch and the other one take the last watch. Wake me at first light."

"You gonna take the watch at first light?" Drake asked.

"No," Breckens said, "we're gonna get goin' at first light. You got a problem with that?"

"Nope," Drake said.

"You?"

"No," Kemp said, "no problem."

"Then get to it," Breckens said, tossing the remnants of his coffee into the fire. "I'm gonna turn in."

Chance couldn't help but wonder where Clint Adams was at that moment and what he was doing. But he wasn't about to just stay in camp and wait for him to come back. He decided to go over to Isaac Brown's tent and have a drink. If the fire went out while he was gone, he'd get it going again.

He thought about what Clint Adams had said about Joe English. Fact was, Chance had often thought about Joe

English the way a man naturally thinks about an attractive woman, but Joe had never given him any indication that she had those thoughts about him, or any man. She was always all businesswoman when he was around—and, he was willing to bet, when he was not around.

When he got to the tent, there were a few spots open at the small bar, and all of the tables were filled with miners. He got the bartender's attention and called him over.

"Hey, Al, gimme a beer, will ya?"

"Comin' up, Buck."

The bartender set a full mug in front of him and said, "Saw the Gunsmith in here earlier with Joe English. That is, I heard he was the Gunsmith. You rode in with him. That true?"

"It's true, all right."

"What's he doin' around here?"

"Keepin' Joe's new partner alive."

"That ain't gonna make Ed Martin too happy."

"Why not?"

"He was real mad at Hector for not sellin' his part of the mine to him," Al said.

"Did Ed have that kind of money?"

"No," the bartender said, "that's why Hector wouldn't sell it to him. Ed wanted to work out a deal but Hector wanted his money all at one time."

"And Joe had that kind of money?"

"In a bank in Denver," Al said. "Left to her by her old man—and who knew he had that kind of cash tucked away?"

This sounded like something Clint Adams should be made aware of.

"You see where Adams went?" he asked.

"Yeah, he left with Joe awhile ago."

"With Joe?"

The bartender nodded, then raised his eyebrows.

"You don't suppose him and Joe— Naw, probably not. Although that would make him one lucky man."

"Yep," Chance said, "it sure would."

# THIRTY-SIX

Joe English's bed was not very wide, and the mattress was not very thick. It was, however, sturdy, built from good wood, and was able to withstand the punishment it was getting from the two people who were rolling around—jumping around—on it.

Joe had obviously been without sex even longer than she had indicated. The first time Clint slid his hand down between her legs, finding her wet and ready, she reacted as if she'd been struck by lightning. Her body spasmed and she bit her lip to keep from screaming. Perversely—if it was perverse to give pleasure—he continued to stroke her there, dipping his fingers into her. She shuddered again and said, "Oh, wait . . ."

He withdrew his hand, leaned over and kissed one of her big breasts, biting the nipple.

"Oh my God," she said, putting her hands up over her head, "it's been so long since a man's touched me . . . but I don't think a man has ever touched me like that!"

"Well," he said, kissing her mouth, "if you liked that, you're going to love this."

He kissed her again, then kissed her chin, her throat, her breasts, and kept working his way down, pausing briefly at

154

J. R. ROBERTS

her belly button and then continuing on down. When he reached the apex between her legs, she gasped but spread her legs wider for him. He kissed the soft flesh of her inner thighs first, working his way closer and closer until finally he touched the tip of his tongue to her wetness. She gasped and jerked, reached for his head and held it as he licked her and sucked her, eventually sliding one finger inside of her and gliding it in and out as he sucked.

He felt her going tense beneath him, moaning out loud, felt her tossing her head from side to side, and, finally, the hands that had been holding him there began to try to pull him away, but he wouldn't have it. He continued to work on her with his tongue and his mouth until she made a high keening, wailing sound, and went incredibly taut beneath him. For a moment it all stopped and he wondered if something had gone wrong, but then she made a sound—almost as if she were shushing him—and her body let go. She began to buck, pushing him away, and then kicking again with her feet to get him away from her. She curled up at the head of the bed and glared at him with flashing eyes.

"What the hell," she said.

"What?"

"Are you crazy?" she asked. "Are you trying to kill me?"

"Joe—"

"That felt too damn good, Clint Adams!" she told him. "I've never felt anything like that before."

"Well, you said you hadn't had sex in a long time."

"I've never had it like this," she said. "I mean—I'm experienced, but not that experienced. But this . . ."

He got to his knees on the bed, his erection jutting out at her. Her eyes went to it and widened.

"And you haven't even done anything to me with that yet!" she said, almost accusingly.

"Joe," he said, "I can leave if you want."

"No!" she snapped, almost desperately. "No, I don't want you to go. I just—I just don't want to have a heart attack."

She looked so comical, all curled up, her hair tossed all over, her eyes glowing hotly, that he had to start laughing. After a moment she started laughing, too, and slowly unfurled until she was stretched out on the bed again.

"Okay," she said, "okay, I'm ready . . ."

"For what?" he asked.

She pointed at his rigid penis and said, "For that!"

"You seem to know your business, too," Ed Martin said to George Markstein.

They had walked away from the desk with the blueprints, and Martin had poured them each a glass of whiskey.

"I'm very familiar with mining," he said, "I just haven't mined turquoise before."

"How did you find out about us?" Martin asked.

"This came across my desk." He reached in his pocket and took out the stone he'd brought with him from home.

Martin took it from him and examined it. "It's rough, spiderweb turquoise," he said.

"From this mine?"

"I'm sure," Martin said. "A lot of the other outfits are still mining copper, and the ones that are mining turquoise are not getting the quality that we're getting."

He handed the stone back.

"How'd you find out it came from us?"

"I did my research, Mr. Martin."

"Ed, please," Martin said. "If we're gonna be working together, you'll have to call me Ed."

"And I'm George."

Ed Martin raised his glass to George Markstein in a toast, and Markstein followed.

"I think we're gonna make a lot of money together, George," he said, clinking his glass against the other man's.

Markstein said, "I certainly hope so, Ed."

# THIRTY-SEVEN

"Wait, wait," Joe said as Clint positioned himself between her legs.

"Whenever you're ready, Joe," he said.

She reached down between her legs and took hold of Clint's penis. She pulled it toward her, touched the spongy head of it to her wet pussy. She rubbed it up and down her wet lips, thoroughly wetting the tip.

"Okay," she said, when they were both wet, "now . . ."

He let her do it. She pulled him to her, then into her. Once the head of his cock entered her, he pushed the rest of the way, but slowly. She gasped, closed her eyes, bit her lip, and eventually he was completely inside her.

"Okay?" he asked.

She smiled with her eyes still closed and said, "Perfect."

He lowered himself over her, then began to move in and out slowly. At the same time he leaned down and licked her breasts, kissed her neck and then her lips. He slipped his tongue into her mouth and she accepted it, sucking it in, letting it out. It was as if he was fucking her with his cock and his tongue at the same time.

"Oooh, oh," she said, lifting her knees, spreading her legs as he began to move faster.

Slowly, her legs came down and wrapped around his waist and she began moving in unison with him, matching his tempo. They both began to grunt and they were really testing just how sturdy the wooden bed frame was.

"Ooh, God, faster, Clint, harder . . ." she implored him.

She was a tall, full-bodied woman and he didn't have to be afraid that he might break her. It was her abstinence from sex that had been causing her to seem almost fragile, but he could feel the power in her legs and thighs, and since she was asking him for more he decided to give it to her. In fact, he decided to lose himself in what he was doing and stop worrying about the effect it might have on her.

He decided to plow her good.

Chance had another beer, decided Clint wasn't coming back to the tent any time soon, and probably wasn't going to come back to camp, either.

"Another one?" the bartender asked him.

"Naw," Chance said. "I'm gonna turn in."

"See ya tomorrow, or you headin' back?"

"I should be around."

Chance waved and left the tent without talking to anyone else. The miners knew him, but he wasn't one of them.

He rebuilt the fire when he got back to the clearing, rolled himself up in his blanket and went to sleep. If Clint came back, it'd probably wake him. If not, he'd sleep 'til about first light, when he usually woke up. The information he had for Clint could wait until then.

Markstein finished his whiskey with Ed Martin and then took his leave to go back to his quarters. The bed was not wide, but he could see it had been well built by someone who knew what he was doing when it came to wood. The thin mattress had been covered with a clean sheet and blanket.

He sat on the bed and took out his gun, which he had not had to use yet. He looked at it, then set it down by the bed. He hoped he'd never have to use it on a man because he had lied to Clint. He didn't know if he'd be able to shoot a man, even to save his own life. It was just not something he had ever considered before.

He was bone tired, but he thought that he had accomplished a lot. He'd made a good impression, he thought, on both Joe English and Ed Martin, and maybe on some of the miners. It was enough for one day, and he had many days ahead of him.

He undressed, keeping on his long johns because it was colder in the mountains than it had been in Kingman, and then covered himself with the sheet and blanket.

After spending the previous night on the hard ground, the bed was so comfortable he fell asleep immediately.

After George Markstein left the office, Ed Martin had another glass of whiskey. He didn't like Markstein, or Clint Adams, because both men had made an impression on Joe. Martin still seethed inside about not having had enough money to buy out Hector Ramirez. The old Mex had insisted on all the money up front and refused to broker some kind of deal with Martin. Now here was George Markstein, willing to sell one percent of the mine, actually willing to practically give away controlling interest in the name of being "fair."

He poured himself another whiskey, thinking that was no way to run a business.

Clint slid his hands beneath Joe's buttocks. It was a position he particularly liked, and he thought she'd like it, too. But once he got her butt lifted off the bed and starting slamming into her, he didn't care what she liked anymore. He started going at her like a thirsty man to a water hole.

She began to pant and grunt, the bed began to make little jumps off the floor, and he started making his own sounds as he felt his release building up in him.

Joe felt her nails rake his back as she was also coming close to going over the edge, but at that moment finding her orgasm was her own problem. He was in the throes of his own and when he exploded, he let loose a bellow that, later, he was convinced had to have been heard throughout the camp.

Especially since it was followed closely by her scream . . .

# THIRTY-EIGHT

Joe English's bed was not wide enough or long enough to share with Clint for the night, so as she lay sleeping—hopefully as exhausted as he was—he dressed and left her small cabin.

He walked through the camp in the middle of the night, alert for any movements. But there weren't any. The miners had all bedded down, and Isaac Brown's tent was dark. By the light of the moon he found his way to the clearing he was sharing with Buck Chance. As he was unrolling his bedroll, Chance roused, tipped his hat up from over his eyes and said, "I didn't expect you to-night."

"I'm bushed," Clint said. "All I want to do is sleep."

"I can imagine."

"What's that mean?" Clint asked, getting comfortable.

"The bartender told me you left with Joe English," Chance said. "I can guess the rest."

"Well . . . she invited me. Said she needed a man who had no connections up here, and would soon be gone."

"Well," Chance said, "far as I can see that describes you to a T."

"Yup." Clint folded his arms across his chest. "I'll see you in the morning."

"I got some information for you."

"Can it wait until morning?"

"Sure," Chance said, pushing his hat back down over his eyes. "I'll get the coffee started."

"Good," Clint said. "Night."

"Good night, Clint . . . you lucky sonofabitch."

Clint woke to the smell of coffee—good, strong trail coffee. He rolled out of his blanket and got to his feet, then staggered to the fire on unsteady legs.

"I think I just may have to take you on the trail with me, Chance," Clint said, accepting a cup of coffee. "This stuff is even better than mine."

"I'll give your offer all the serious thought it deserves, Clint," Chance said. "Are you interested in what I was gonna tell you last night?"

Clint took a big swallow of coffee first, then said, "Yeah, sure. Whataya got?"

"It's about Ed Martin," Chance said, and then relayed the story about Martin he'd gotten from Al, the bartender.

"So Martin really shouldn't be welcoming George here with open arms," Clint said when Chance was done.

"Or even worse."

"You know Martin," Clint said. "Is he capable of hiring someone to kill George?"

"I don't know him all that well, but I think anybody's capable of havin' somebody murdered," Chance said. "What's it take, some money?"

"And somebody who wants the job, but there are plenty of those types around."

"Like this fella Breckens?"

"He should be here any time now," Clint said. "Maybe we'll find out something from him."

"How are we gonna do that?"

"Easy," Clint said. "We'll just ask him."


"Why are we stopping here?" Kemp asked. "Ain't the Blue Lady just up ahead?"

"We're gonna dismount here and you two are gonna wait," Breckens said. "I gotta go in and talk to the man who's payin' me."

"Payin' you?" Drake asked. "Ain't he payin' us?"

"No," Breckens said. "He's payin' me and I'm payin' you. See the difference?"

He dismounted, followed by the other two men.

"Watch my horse."

"Okay," Kemp said.

"Don't go anywhere," he said. "I don't want you two to be seen."

"Okay," Drake said. "We get it, Carl."

Breckens studied them for a few moments, wondering if the moment he was gone they'd hightail it over to Isaac Brown's tent. Finally, he left.


Ed Martin looked up from the desk when there was a knock at the back door. When he opened it and saw Carl Breckens, he flipped.

"What the hell are you doing here?" Martin demanded.

"Relax," Breckens said. "Nobody saw me. I just wanted to check and see if I still have a job."

"You do," Martin said, "but only because I'd never find anyone else at such short notice."

"Okay, so you still want them dead."

"If you think you can get it done, Breckens. So far your record is not that good."

"Don't you worry about my record," Breckens said. "Just have the rest of my money ready!"

"You do the job and you'll get your money," Martin said. "Now get away from here before somebody sees you."

"Next time you see me you'll be payin' me," Breckens said.

"I hope so," Martin said, and he really did.

# THIRTY-NINE

"Now you want us to go into camp?" Kemp asked.

"Adams doesn't know you," Breckens said. "He's never seen you, so you'll be able to move around freely."

"I thought he ain't never seen you either?" Drake asked.

"Well, I ain't sure about that," Breckens said. "And maybe Edwards told him who I was and described me."

"Well, he coulda described us, too," Jeff Kemp said. "Didja ever think of that?"

"Just go into the camp of the Blue Lady," Breckens said. "They got a tent that serves whiskey."

"I could use a whiskey," Kemp said.

"Me, too," Drake said.

"There ya go," Breckens said. "So this is perfect for the two of you."

"And what do we do about Adams?" Kemp asked.

"Just locate him," Breckens said. "And see if you can locate Markstein, too."

"Who's he?" Drake asked.

"I told you, the man from the East who bought into the mine," Breckens said. "He's the one we need to get rid of."

"Not the Gunsmith?" Kemp asked.

"Only if he gets in the way," Breckens said. "Look, just drift in, have a few drinks—"

"The saloon'll be open this early?" Drake asked, surprised.

"It's not a saloon, just a tent, and yes, it'll be open," Breckens said. "Some of the miners work later, so they have to drink earlier. Isaac Brown knows that, so he serves liquor early."

"Maybe it wouldn't be so bad to be a miner," Drake said to Kemp.

"Well, think about gettin' a job after you finish this one," Breckens said. "Just get goin'."

"What about you?" Kemp asked.

"Don't worry, I'll be around."

The two men mounted up and headed into the mining camp. Breckens looked after them, shaking his head. If he could just use them to attract the Gunsmith's attention, he'd be able to take care of George Markstein and get the rest of his money from Ed Martin.

Clint and Chance finished their coffee with some bacon and beans Chance still had left, and then doused their fire. There were other smells in the air, cooking from other fires in the area, and from the miner's mess.

"What about the tent?" Clint asked. "Do they ever serve food?"

"They put out some hard-boiled eggs for the miners," Chance said, "but that's about it."

"Well," Clint said, "I'm going to go over and see George."

"If he's satisfied with his situation, will you be headin' out?" Chance asked. "Back to Kingman?"

"We've still got to deal with this fella Breckens and whoever he's got with him," Clint said.

"Do you even know what he looks like?"

"If he's the man who was following us in town, I caught a glimpse of him once or twice," Clint explained, "but mostly I just have Edwards's description to work from."

"And the other two?"

"I've got nothing on them."

"And it could be more than two, right?"

"I don't think Edwards was lying about that," Clint said. "I think we're looking for three men."

"So we go lookin' for three riders."

"If Breckens has any kind of smarts," Clint said, "he'll send the other two in first, as a distraction."

"So we need to look for two men?"

"No," Clint said, "I need to look for two men, you need to stick by George—unless you want to face the two."

"I'll take one and leave two to you," Chance said. "You've got more experience."

"Okay then," Clint said. "Let's go and see George, and on the way you can tell me what a typical day up here is like."

"Well," Chance said, "for one thing, you can drink any time up here . . ."

Clint and Chance knocked on the door of the cabin that was serving as Markstein's quarters. The man opened the door, looking haggard and anything but rested.

"I didn't sleep very well," he confessed as he let them in. "I'm going to have to do something about getting a good mattress."

"What's on your schedule for today, George?" Clint asked.

"Well, breakfast first, and then I have to meet with Ed Martin and Joe English to discuss some business."

"Okay," Clint said, "Buck is going to go with you today, until we're sure that you're safe."

"And you?"

"I'm going to be the one who goes out and makes sure you're safe."

# FORTY

Normally Clint would have been surprised to find a bunch of men drinking in a saloon before nine a.m. Buck Chance's explanation kept that from being the case when he walked into the Tent. That, he'd discovered, was what everyone called Isaac Brown's place. As he walked in, he recalled it being said that two men had opened the Tent. Idly, he wondered who Brown's partner was in the endeavor.

"Ah, Mr. Adams," Brown said, approaching Clint. "What can my humble establishment offer you? A drink, or perhaps some supplies?" He was still dressed the way Clint had seen him the night before—dark suit and a tie, expensive watch chain hanging from his vest—but it was a clean suit. Clint wondered how many of them he owned, and how hard they were to keep clean around the mines.

"Do you serve coffee?"

"Best in the area," Brown said. "Come with me to the bar. I was just going to have a cup myself."

"No whiskey for you in the morning?"

"I'm not a miner," Brown said. "It's still too early for me."

When they got to the bar, Brown told the bartender to bring them each a coffee. The three men standing at the bar and the four seated at the various tables were all miners, who looked Clint over curiously—either because they didn't know who he was, or because they did. He wondered if any of them were from the Blue Lady.

"So tell me, how much longer do you plan on staying around the mines?" Brown asked.

"Not much longer," Clint said. "Just until I'm sure George Markstein is safe up here."

"That word, safe, it's very relative."

"Well, I meant safe from an impending threat," Clint said. "What happens after I leave is out of my hands."

"So who do you think you're keeping him safe from?"

"I'm looking for three men," Clint said. "Two will come in together, followed by the third awhile later."

"Why won't they come in together?"

"Because the first man will use the other two as bait."

"For what?"

"Not what," Clint said. "Who. Me."

"And how is it you know this?"

"I don't know it," Clint said, "but it's logical. It's what I'd do."

"So you're dealing with a smart man?"

"More crafty than smart," Clint said. "In fact, I don't think he's very smart at all."

"Well," Brown said, "then I guess it's a good thing you're craftier."

"I'm going to hang around here awhile, Mr. Brown," Clint said. "When they do ride in, there aren't going to be many places they can go."

"First, please call me Isaac," Brown said, "and second, I hope you're not planning on killing anyone in my place."

"I'm not planning on killing anyone, period," Clint said, "but it may not be my call."

"I understand. Well, I'm afraid I have some work to do. You stay around as long as you like."

"Thank you."

Brown carried his coffee to the back of the tent, where he went through a flap to a small office he had carved out for himself. Once there, he put his coffee cup down on his desk and left the tent by the back flap.

Since it was not unusual for Brown to be seen walking through the camp, he made no pretense about where he was going. He made his way to the headquarters of the Blue Lady Mine and entered without knocking. He knew he'd find Ed Martin there, because the man rarely slept.

"Must be somethin' important to bring you over here, Isaac," Ed Martin said.

"Who the hell did you hire?" Brown demanded. "First Markstein was not supposed to even get here and then when he does he brings the Gunsmith with him."

"Relax," Martin said. "The job will get done."

"Oh, yeah? Well, right now Adams is over at my place waiting for your killer to arrive with his two friends. He's got their every move figured out ahead of time, Ed."

Martin put down the blueprints he was holding and gave his full attention to his silent partner. Rather, it was he who was the silent partner. Everyone knew there were two men behind the Tent, but no one knew Martin was the second.

"Tell me," he said, "everything."

When Joe English woke, she was feeling pleasantly exhausted. Certain parts of her body were still tingling, and if she closed her eyes she could still feel Clint Adams's hands and mouth on her. She shivered, then opened her eyes and shook off the feeling. It had been a wonderful night, one she'd been needing for a long time—so long, in fact, that she had actually found herself considering one of Isaac Brown's many advances. In the end, though, she had been smart to hold out for someone like Clint Adams. No, actually, it was a good thing she had held out specifically for Clint Adams.

The night with him should be enough to hold her until the time her urge became unbearable. Maybe she should just pick out one miner to be her regular lover, keep him on the job until she tired of him and then move on.

No, talk about unsound business practices, that would be the unsoundest of all.

She got up, washed herself and got dressed for breakfast.

Now that she'd had sex, the next urge she was going to have to satisfy was for a long, hot bath.

# FORTY-ONE

When Isaac Brown stopped talking, Ed Martin opened a desk drawer, took out a gun belt and strapped it on.

"What are you doing?" Brown demanded.

"We might have to take a hand in this ourselves, Isaac," Martin said. "I suggest you put on your gun."

"Are you crazy?" Isaac Brown asked. "I don't have a gun!"

Martin reached across the desk and grabbed Brown by the jacket lapel.

"Then you'd better get one."

"I thought we hired somebody for this."

"Well, apparently he's not going to get the job done—not with Adams predicting his every move."

"So what do you expect us to do?"

"Well," Martin said, releasing Brown, "if our man Breckens is going to use his two men as a distraction, then maybe we'll just do the same thing to him."

At that moment the door opened and Joe English stepped in.

"Well," she said as Martin backed off Brown, "what can you two boys be discussing at this hour of the morning?"

174 J. R. ROBERTS

Isaac Brown didn't know what to say, but Ed Martin was quick off the mark.

"Isaac is worried about Clint Adams hanging around his place," Martin said. "He thinks there might be trouble."

"I don't think Clint is here looking for trouble, do you, Ed?" she asked.

"I don't think a man like Clint Adams has to look for trouble, Joe," Martin said. "I think it just finds him."

"Is that why you're wearing a gun today?"

"We have a dynamic around here we don't usually have," he explained. "At any minute somebody could get it into their head to make a try for Mr. Adams. That's why I've suggested that Isaac wear a gun, too."

"Isaac?" she asked, laughing. "Do you even own a gun?"

Brown didn't like the idea of Joe laughing at him, so he said, "Of course I have a gun. Every man has a gun."

"Why don't you go back to your place and put it on, Isaac," Martin suggested.

"Yeah, yeah," Brown said, "why don't I do that."

He left, walking past Joe without saying a word, which she found odd. Isaac Brown never missed an opportunity to make a sexual comment to her.

"What's going on, Ed?" she asked.

"I explained—"

"No," she said, shaking her head, "there's something else."

Before he could open his mouth to comment, the door opened again and both George Markstein and Buck Chance entered.

"Are we interrupting?" Markstein said.

Ed Martin thought this would be perfect if only Joe and Chance weren't around.

"Of course not, George," he said. "Come on in. Good morning. Hello, Buck."

"Ed."

"You acting as George's bodyguard today?"

"Something like that."

"Well, you can leave him here," Martin said. "He'll certainly be in good hands."

"That's okay," Chance said. "I got nowhere else to be right now."

Markstein looked at Joe and at Ed Martin and said, "Shall we get down to business, then?"

"Of course." Martin was itching to draw his gun and put a bullet in Markstein's brain. "Why don't we?"

Isaac Brown made his way back to his tent and entered his office by way of the back flap. He hadn't actually been telling Martin the truth. He did own a gun, but he was always afraid he'd shoot his own foot off. That's why he had employed the bartender, Al Conroy, who had abilities not only with whiskey bottles but also with guns.

That was it, he had to call Al in and explain things in such a way that the man would be ready at a moment's notice to use the gun he had behind the bar.

Isaac Brown reentered the commercial part of his tent just in time to see two strangers, both wearing guns, enter through the front flap.

Christ, was he too late?

Clint saw the two men enter, and the hair on the back of his neck stood up, a sure sign of things to come. They were both armed, holster leather worn. Their guns were unremarkable, but the men looked like they'd used them before.

Not smart enough to realize that Clint was the only man in the place who didn't look like a miner—except for the bartender—the two men approached the bar and ordered whiskey. They were standing just feet away from Clint.

Clint turned and leaned on the bar, watching the two men, listening to the bartender talk to them.

"You boys are new," he said, pouring them each a drink.

"Just passing through," Paul Drake said.

"Here?" Al asked, laughing. "On the way to where?"

"Why don't you mind your own business?" Kemp asked.

"Hey, pal," Al said, "I'm a bartender. This is my business."

"Forgive my friend, here," Drake said. "He's got no manners. Truth of the matter is, we're lookin' for somebody."

"Oh? And who might that be?"

Before anyone could say another word, Clint straightened up and said, "Me."

# FORTY-TWO

Jeff Kemp and Paul Drake both turned their heads slowly to look at the man who had spoken.

"I'm Clint Adams," Clint said, "and you men were sent in by Carl Breckens, weren't you?"

"How did you know th—" Kemp started, but Drake nudged him quiet.

"Mister, we don't know what you're talkin' about," Drake said. "We just came in for a drink."

"Right," Clint said, "this early in the morning and just passing through . . . to where?"

Neither man was able to think of a viable answer. The sudden tension in the room caused the miners who were there to back away from the bar and their tables to the general store side of the tent, where there was cover. Al, the bartender, stayed where he was, his hand near the six-gun he kept under the bar.

Isaac Brown remained where he was, watching carefully. If Adams gunned down these two men, he was going out the back way to let Ed Martin know what had happened.

* * *

Carl Breckens watched the two men go into the tent, then made his way through the camp toward the main headquarters of the Blue Lady Mine. He'd neglected to find out from Ed Martin what cabin Markstein was in. With any luck Martin would still be there.

Clint turned to face away from the bar and toward the two men.

"Breckens has thrown you to the wolves, boys," Clint said. "While you're here getting killed, he thinks he's going to get the job done, get paid and not have to pay you. Don't you see?"

"There's two of us, mister," Drake said, pushing Kemp away from him so there was some distance between them.

"Paul—" Kemp said.

"We can do this, Jeff," Drake said. "It means a lot of money,"

"You can't collect money," Clint told them, "and you damn sure can't spend it if you're dead."

Martin, Joe and Markstein had their heads together, bent over the desk, studying blueprints. Chance had elected to take a chair over by the other desk. He was tremendously bored when the door opened and Carl Breckens walked in. Chance didn't know he was Breckens at the time. All he knew was that he was a man wearing a gun.

"Martin, you didn't tell me—" Breckens stopped short when he saw all the people in the room.

Martin reacted immediately. He pushed Markstein away from him, shouted, "Look out, George," and drew his gun.

Breckens, surprised, drew his gun as a pure reflex, but he was too late. Martin pulled the trigger and shot him in the chest. Chance, shocked into action, jumped up and drew his gun as Breckens staggered backwards out the door, pulling the trigger of his gun and firing one shot.

"What the hell—" Chance said, turning to face Martin. They pointed their guns at each other . . .

The two men might have given it up if it hadn't been for the shots. As they all heard them, they all moved.

Kemp and Drake went for their guns, leaving Clint no choice. He drew and fired twice, killing them both.

Al grabbed his gun from beneath the bar and brought it up just as Clint turned to him.

"Put it down," Clint said.

Al released the gun as if it were hot and it clattered to the bar top.

"Hey, hey, I was just gonna try to help, man," Al said.

Clint swept the gun off the bar with one arm, sending it skittering across the floor toward Isaac Brown. Then he bent to check the two men to be sure they were dead.

As the gun came sliding across the floor to Isaac Brown, he made a spur-of-the-moment decision. As Clint bent over the men, Brown picked up the gun, took a few steps toward Clint and raised it.

Al saw what Brown was going to do and shouted, "Hey, no boss," thinking that Brown misinterpreted what had taken place.

Clint didn't need the warning, though. He heard Brown's steps behind him, turned and fired by instruct. The bullet struck Brown in the chest on the right side. His arm immediately lost all feeling and the gun dropped from his hand.

"What the hell—" Clint said, but he didn't have time to figure out what had happened. He turned and ran from the Tent toward the Blue Lady Mining Company headquarters.

"Take it easy," Chance said to Martin, lowering his gun.

For a moment Martin considered firing again, but instead he lowered his weapon as well.

"I'll go out and see if he's dead," Chance said.

"What happened?" Markstein asked.

Joe, who had frozen in place next to Martin, said, "What the hell was that?"

But Martin wasn't listening. He rushed across the room, gun in hand. If Breckens was still alive, he might say something to Chance.

As Martin reached the door, he saw Chance leaning over Breckens who, indeed, was still alive. Unsure as to whether he should shoot Chance first and then Breckens, or the other way around, he raised his gun. If Breckens talked, he'd have to kill them both anyway. The order didn't matter.

Clint was acting on pure instinct, because there was no time to ask questions. When he saw Buck Chance leaning over a fallen man and Ed Martin in the doorway raising a gun, he didn't stop to consider who the man was going to shoot. It was enough to see that he was about to.

Clint raised his gun and fired once.

# FORTY-THREE

After Clint had told his story to the sheriff back in Kingman, the man said, "Okay, let me get this straight. Ed Martin and Isaac Brown were partners, and they wanted George Markstein killed so they could take over his half of the mine."

"Right."

"What made Martin think he'd get that half?" the lawman asked. "I'm not an expert on that kind of law, but wouldn't it go to the surviving partner? Joe English?"

"I suppose so," Clint said. "I don't think he thought that far ahead."

Cafferty shook his head and said, "It's enough of a surprise finding out that Martin and Brown were partners. How does Joe English feel about all this?"

"She and Markstein are getting along well," Clint said. "He's going to be a very hands-on owner, so I don't think they'll miss Ed Martin very much."

"Guess you musta felt pretty bad about shooting Isaac until you found out the whole story."

"I relied on my instinct, which told me I was in danger. I didn't feel bad at all."

"Oh, well . . . I suppose Buck Chance will back your story?"

"He will," Clint said. "With his dying breath Breckens told Buck that Ed Martin had hired him."

"Well, I don't think you need to hang around town much longer, then," Kingman said. "I'll get a hold of Buck and I'm sure he'll back you."

"Much obliged, Sheriff," Clint said. "I would like to get moving. Been around here much too long as it is."

Cafferty walked Clint out, thinking that the Gunsmith had been around long enough to kill five men—counting Mike Dolan. That was long enough for him, too.

Clint's horse was outside, and he grabbed the reins from the hitching post.

"I heard a story from the mine," Cafferty said.

"What kind of story?"

"Somebody came to town with a story about one percent of the mine?" he asked. "Apparently that was all that separated the two partners?"

"That's right."

"So what'd they do?"

"Markstein was going to sell one percent to Joe so they'd be even partners, but instead he gave two percent of the mine away to somebody else."

"Really?" Cafferty asked. "Who'd he give it to?"

Clint smiled at Cafferty and said, "I'm afraid that's between him and whoever he gave it to, Sheriff."

Watch for

**WILDFIRE**

313th novel in the exciting GUNSMITH series
from Jove

*Coming in January!*

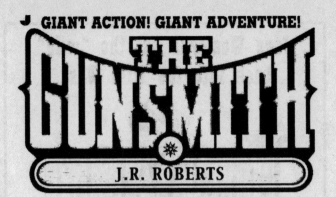

GIANT ACTION! GIANT ADVENTURE!

# THE GUNSMITH

## J.R. ROBERTS

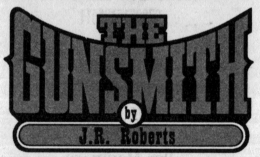

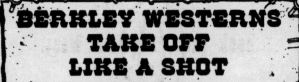